FAREWELL TO SHADY GLADE

written and illustrated by BILL PEET

HOUGHTON MIFFLIN COMPANY BOSTON

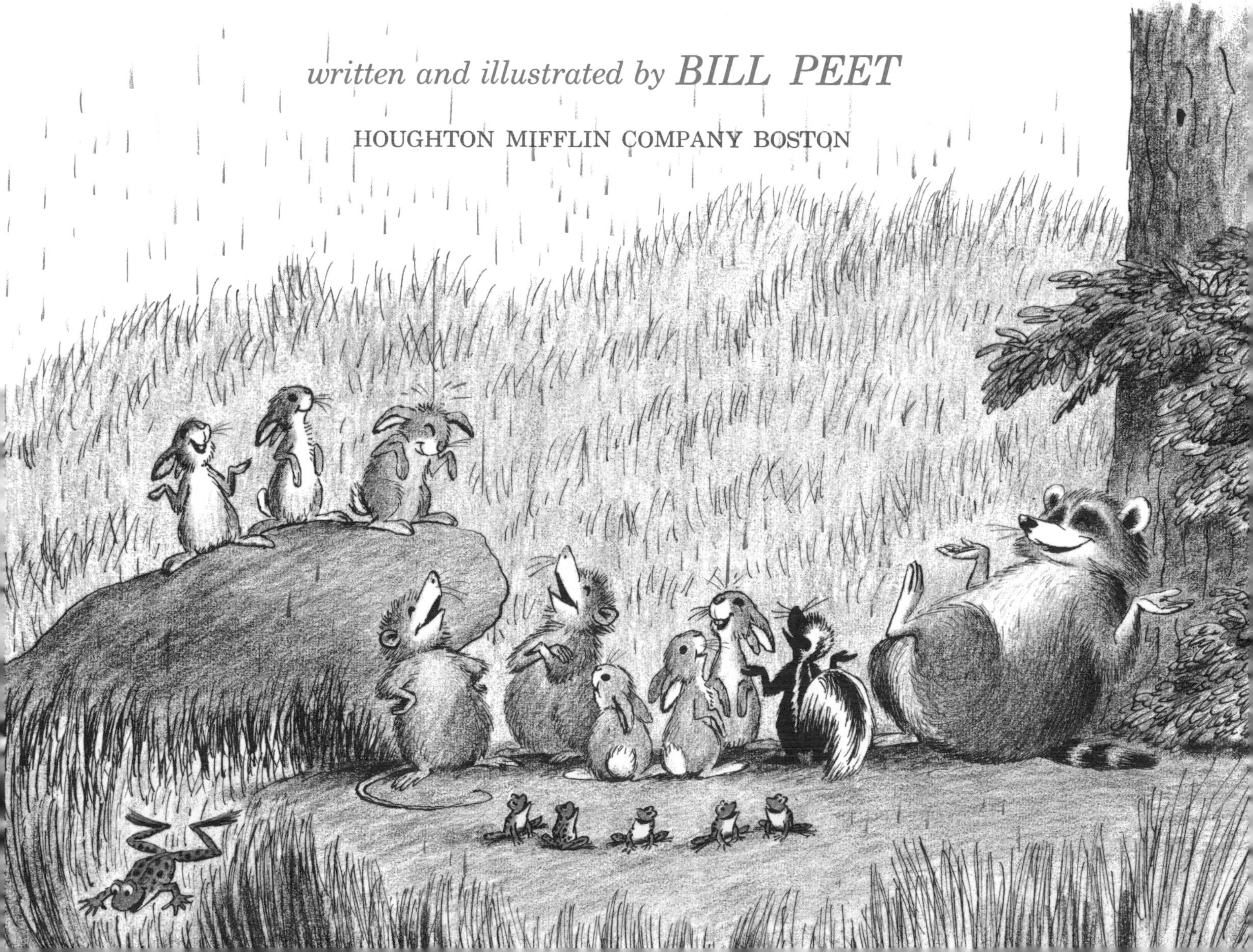

To

RACHEL CARSON

with the hope that the new generation
will carry on her all-important work
toward preserving what is left
of our natural world.

ISBN 0-395-18975-6 (rnf.)
ISBN 0-395-31128-4 (Sandpiper pbk.)

Printed in the United States of America

WOZ 20 19 18

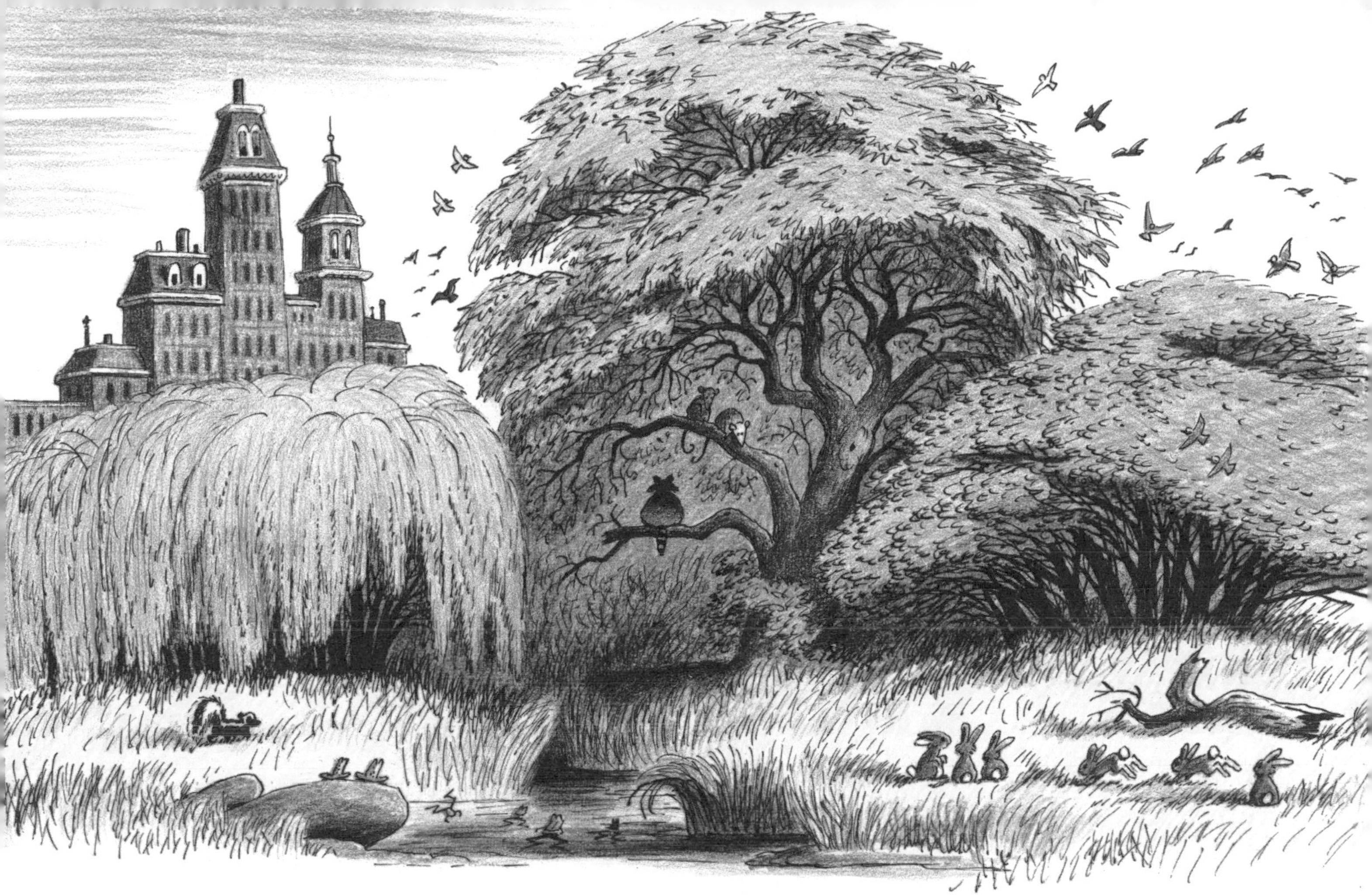

SHADY GLADE was a towering sycamore and a cluster of willows and cottonwoods along the banks of a winding creek. Early every spring hundreds of birds flocked into the treetops to build their nests, raise their young, and then go their way at the end of summer.

The year round population of the glade was no more than sixteen: half a dozen rabbits, a pair of possums, a single skunk, five green frogs, one bullfrog, and an old raccoon. They lived there together in a peaceful neighborly fashion. These simple woodland creatures were content to believe that nothing could ever spoil their quiet little world. They hardly noticed the big city looming up to the sky way off in the distance.

Then one spring day there came a deep rumbling sound.

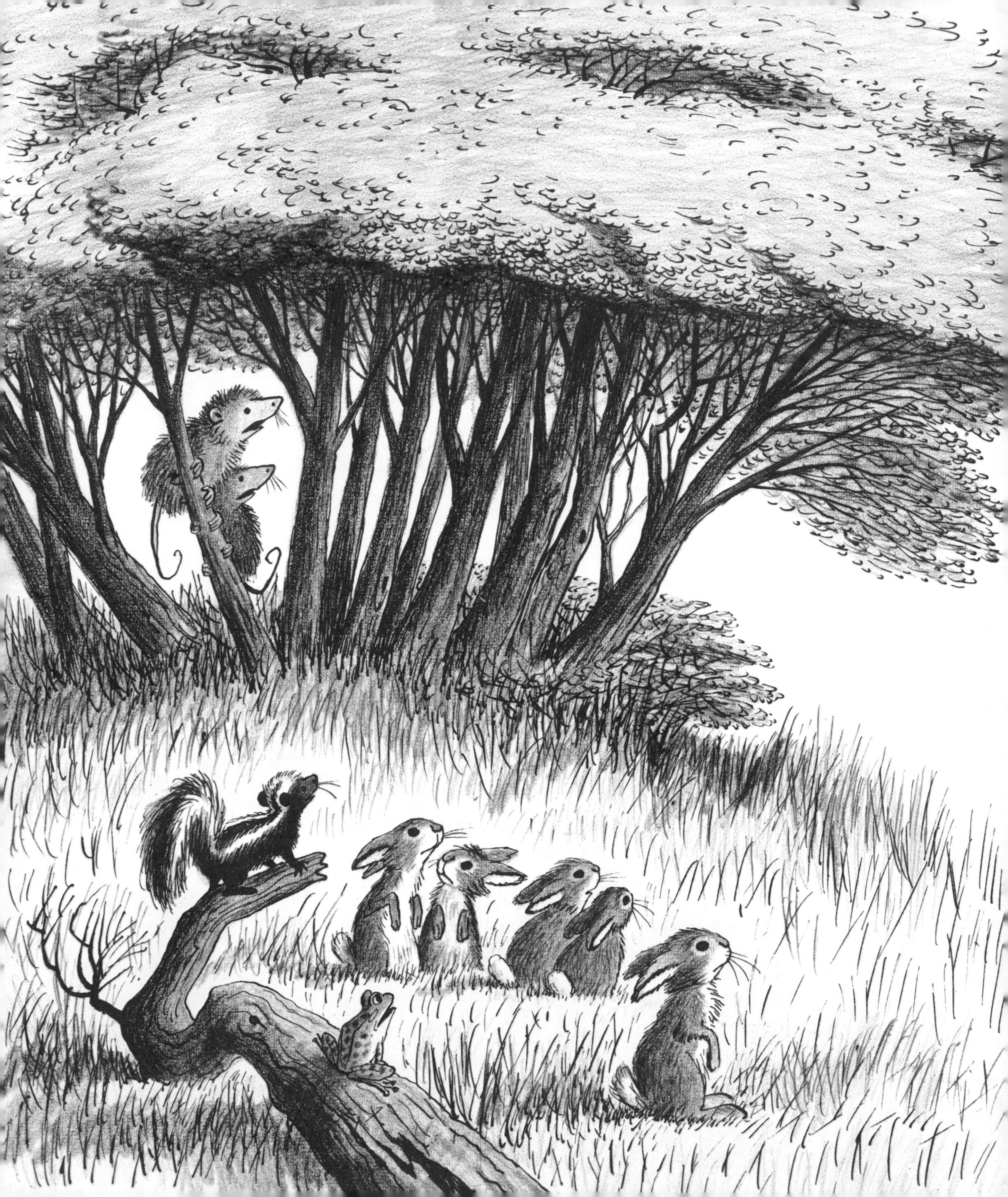

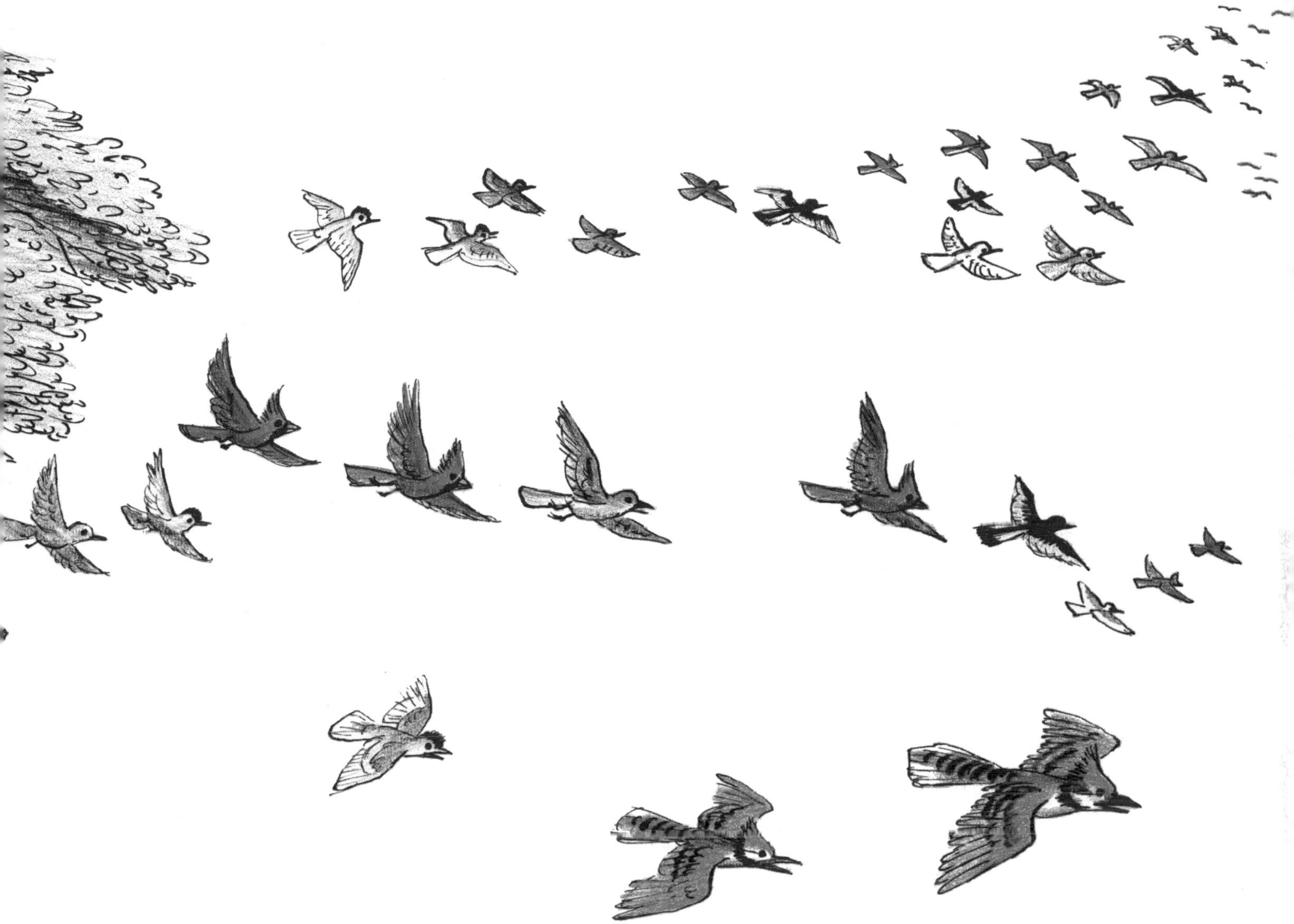

The rumbling began early in the morning and continued on through the day, then along toward evening it suddenly stopped. Each day it grew louder and more ominous and by the end of the week the rumbling shook the whole glade. The trees trembled to their very roots and the creek shivered in its banks. The birds stopped in the middle of their songs and nestbuilding, then without a word, took off in a fluttering flurry and went streaking out of the glade in all directions.

The sudden departure of the birds caused great alarm among the other creatures of the glade. They wondered whether it was merely the noise that had scared them away, or if there was a threat of real danger. They quickly gathered in a frightened group around the wise old raccoon, anxious to hear what he thought about the mysterious rumbling.

"It's not a train," said the old fellow peering up at the railroad trestle that straddled the creek, "and there hasn't been a cloud in the sky for weeks, so the rumbling can't be thunder."

"A little noise never hurt anyone," boomed the bullfrog.

"Just the same," warned the raccoon, "we'd better find out what it is." And he went scrambling up the towering sycamore, all the way up the twisting trunk to the very top branches.

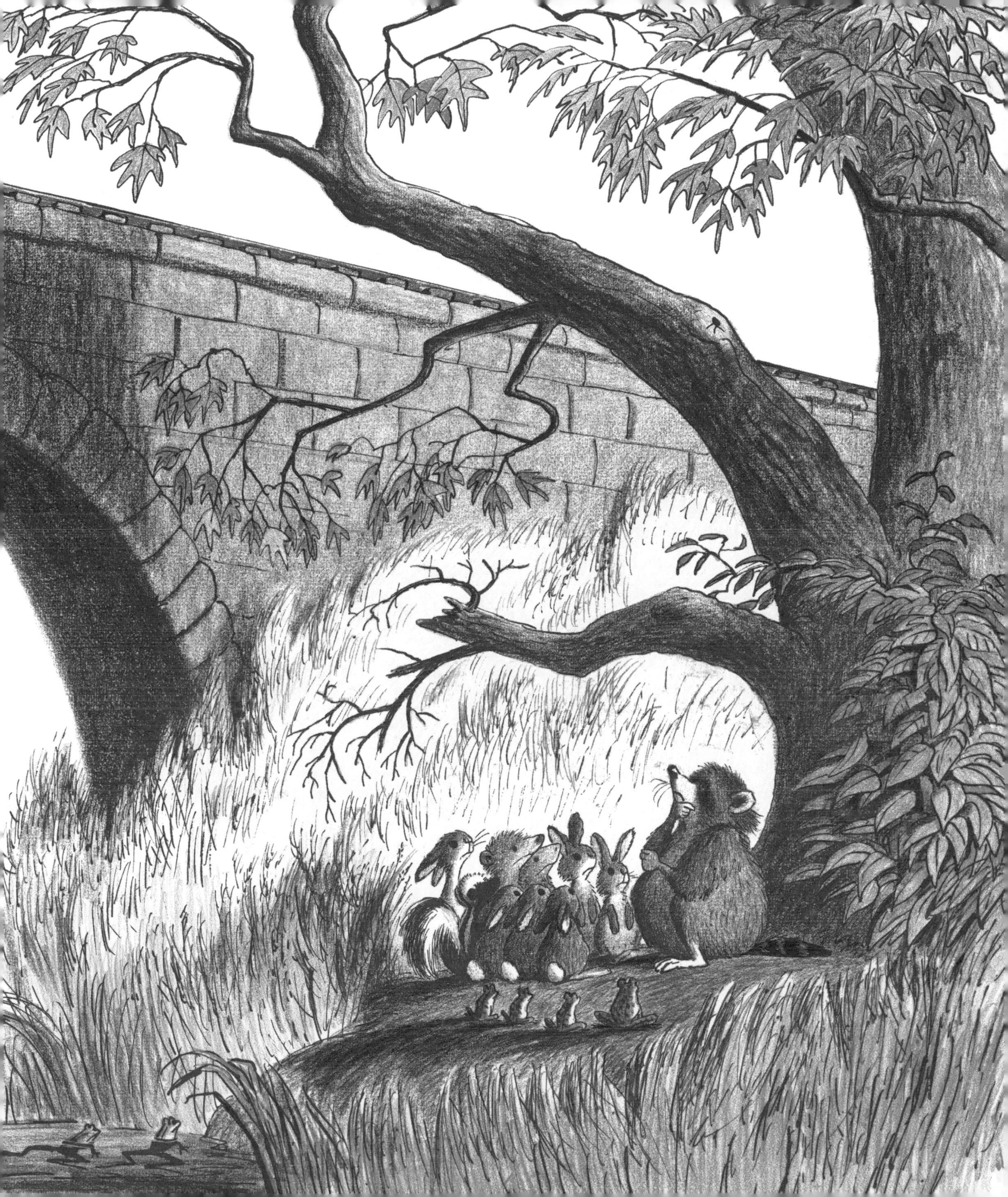

Then just beyond a hill not more than fifty yards to the east he spotted the rumblers. Monstrous machines gouging out whole clumps of trees in one scoop, a ton of earth in one bite, leaving nothing but their giant tracks on the barren ground. And they were heading straight for Shady Glade!

"We're in for it," muttered the raccoon as he scurried down the tree to rejoin his friends.

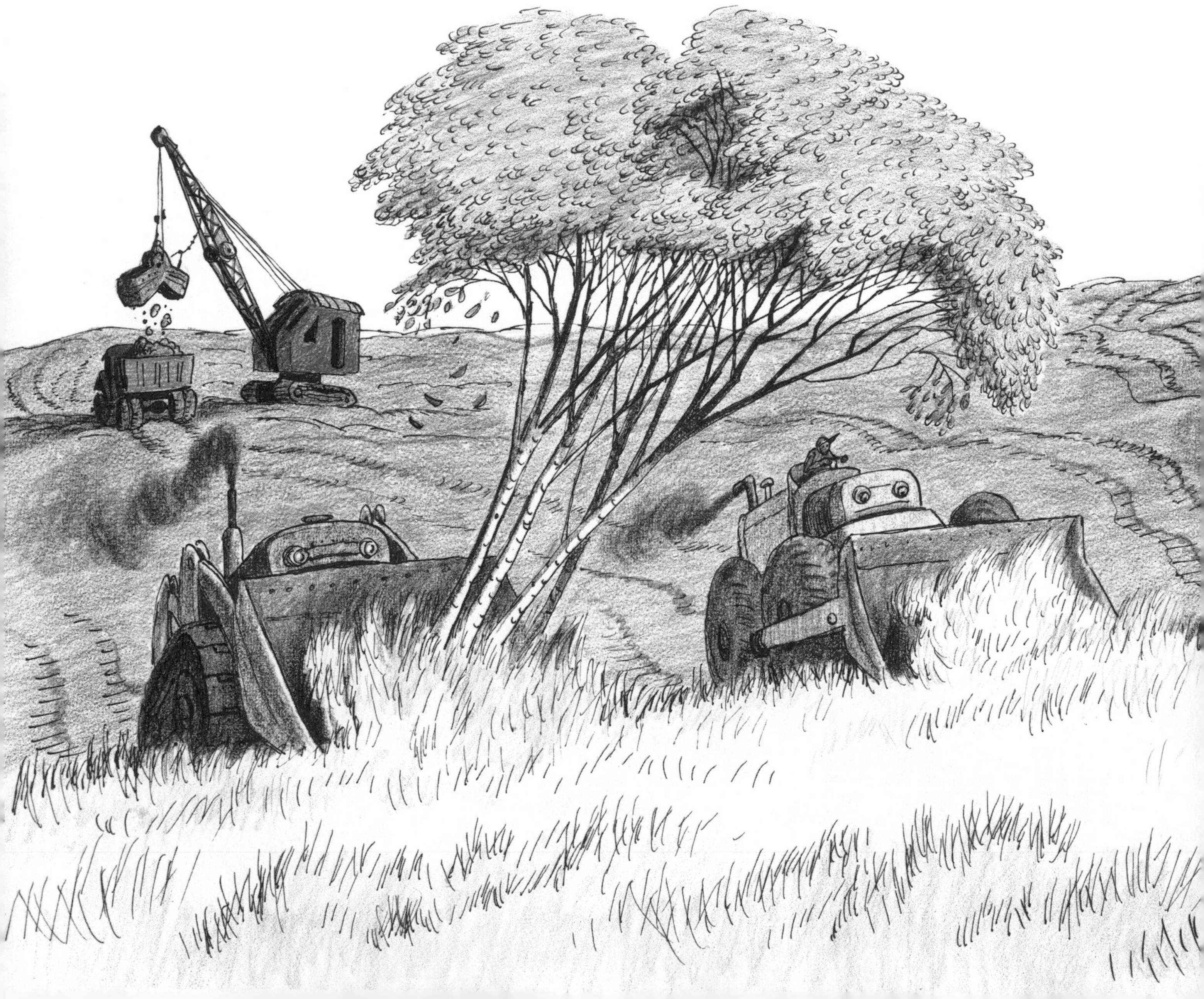

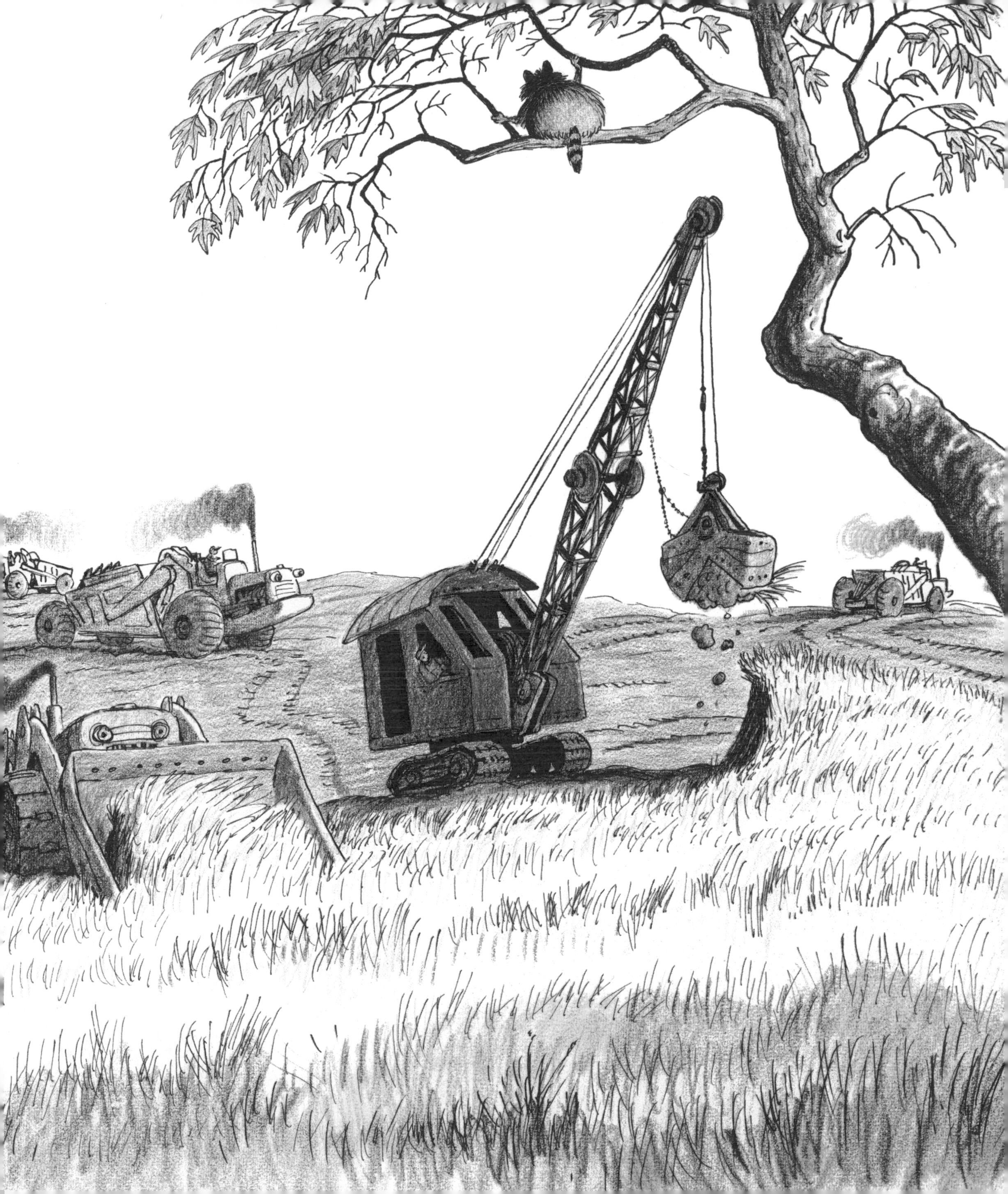

He tried his best to describe the gigantic mechanical monsters, but all his words and frantic gestures proved to be useless. The blank befuddled faces gave no sign of understanding. Then with a long forefinger he attempted to draw one of the machines in the soft earth, a hodgepodge of scratchy lines which merely confused them all the more.

"Oh well," he sighed, "the monsters will stop work before nightfall. Then you can all go see for yourselves."

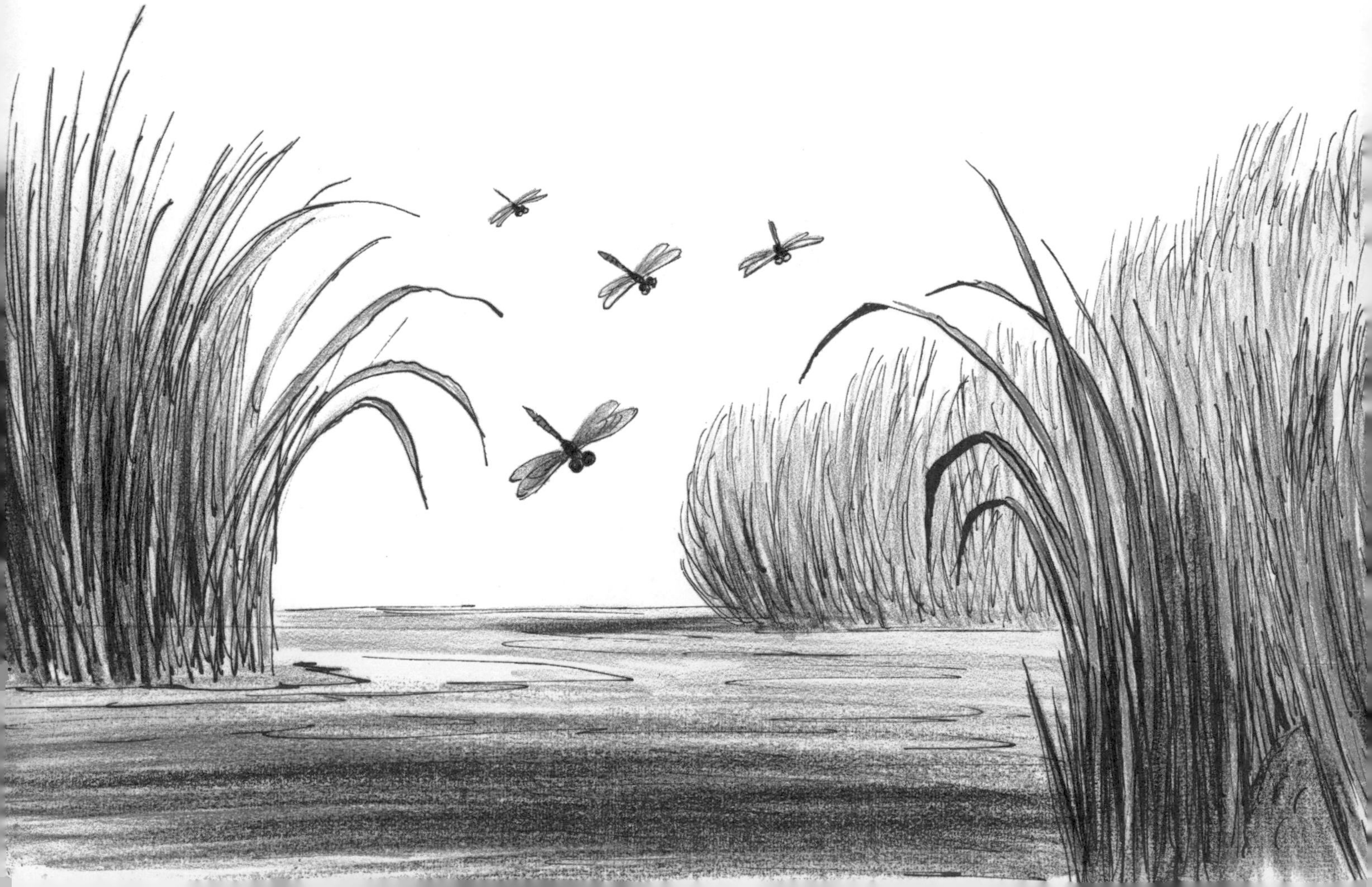

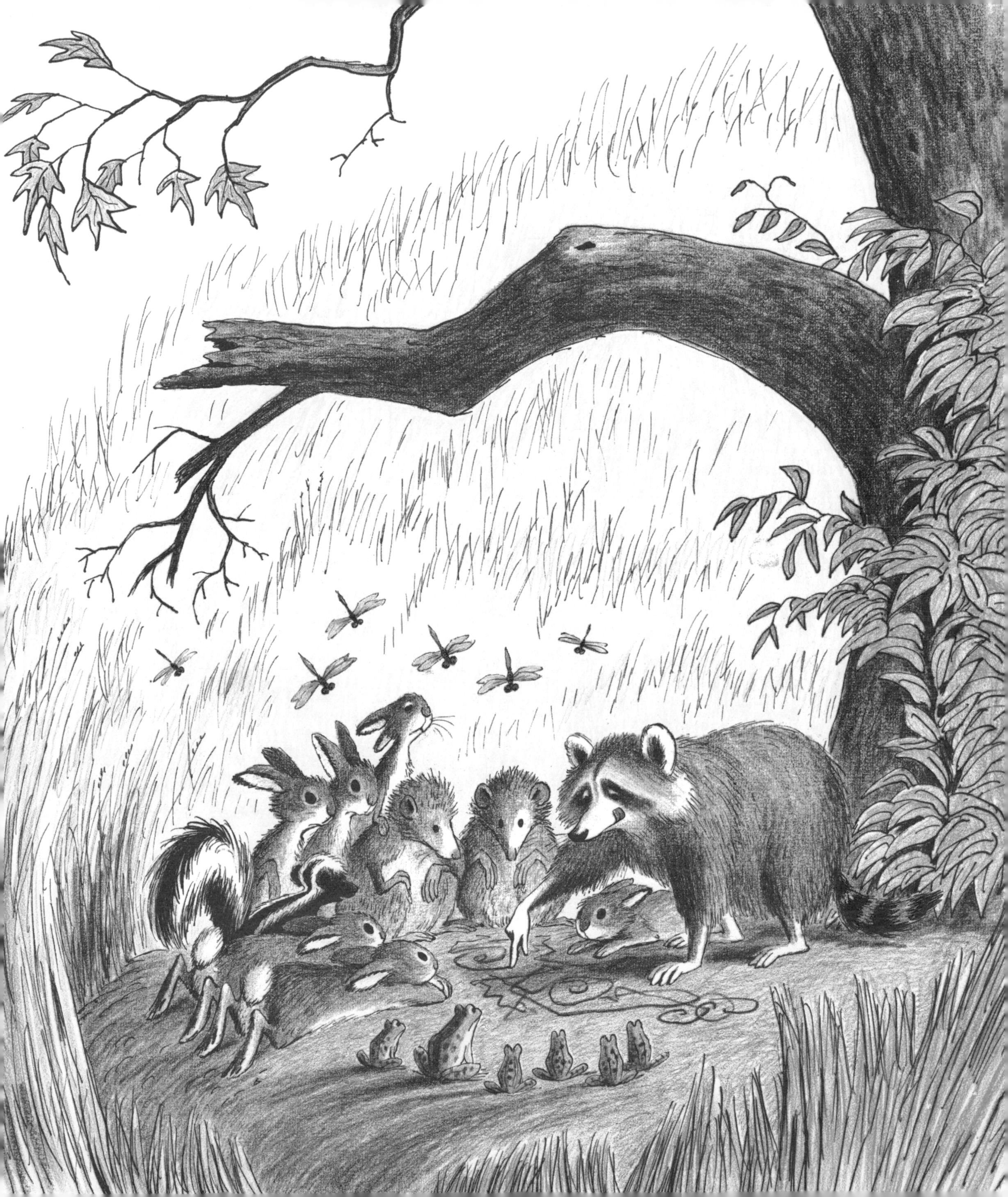

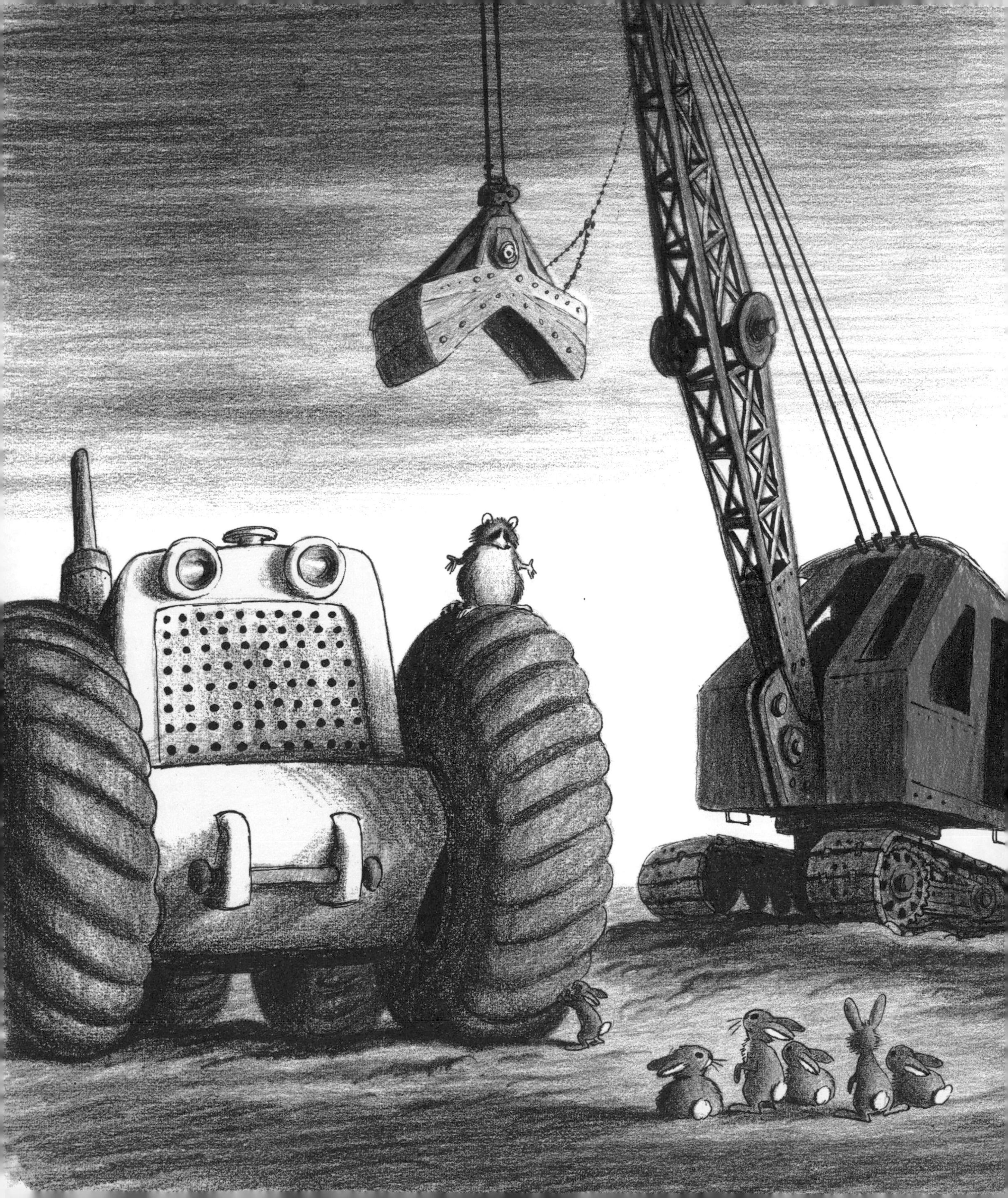

Along toward evening after the rumbling had stopped the raccoon led his little animal friends out of the glade and across a grassy meadow. When they caught sight of the huge mechanical monsters they stopped dead in their tracks trembling with fright. All but the brave raccoon. He waddled straight for the nearest machine and went climbing up a giant wheel to perch on the top.

"Have no fear," he said. "They can't budge an inch without their drivers. Right now they're helpless."

"Then this is the time to attack," said the bravest of the rabbits. And baring his large front teeth he leaped at a giant tire.

The raccoon shook his head. "It's no use. You won't find any soft spots. The brutes are indestructible, all powerful, and there's no stopping them. Shady Glade is doomed."

"What'll we do?" they all wailed at once.

"Nothing at all tonight," replied the raccoon, "but I suspect we have a long day ahead of us tomorrow, so you'd better get some sleep."

There was no sleep that night for the old raccoon. He sat up in the sycamore wide awake trying to find an answer to their problem. Of one thing he was certain, they must leave Shady Glade. Where they would go he had no idea. He had spent his whole life in the glade and the trip out to view the machines was the farthest he'd ever ventured. The outside world was a big mystery. The raccoon only knew there was an awful lot of it. So he figured there was a very good chance of finding another Shady Glade out there somewhere. At least they must take that chance.

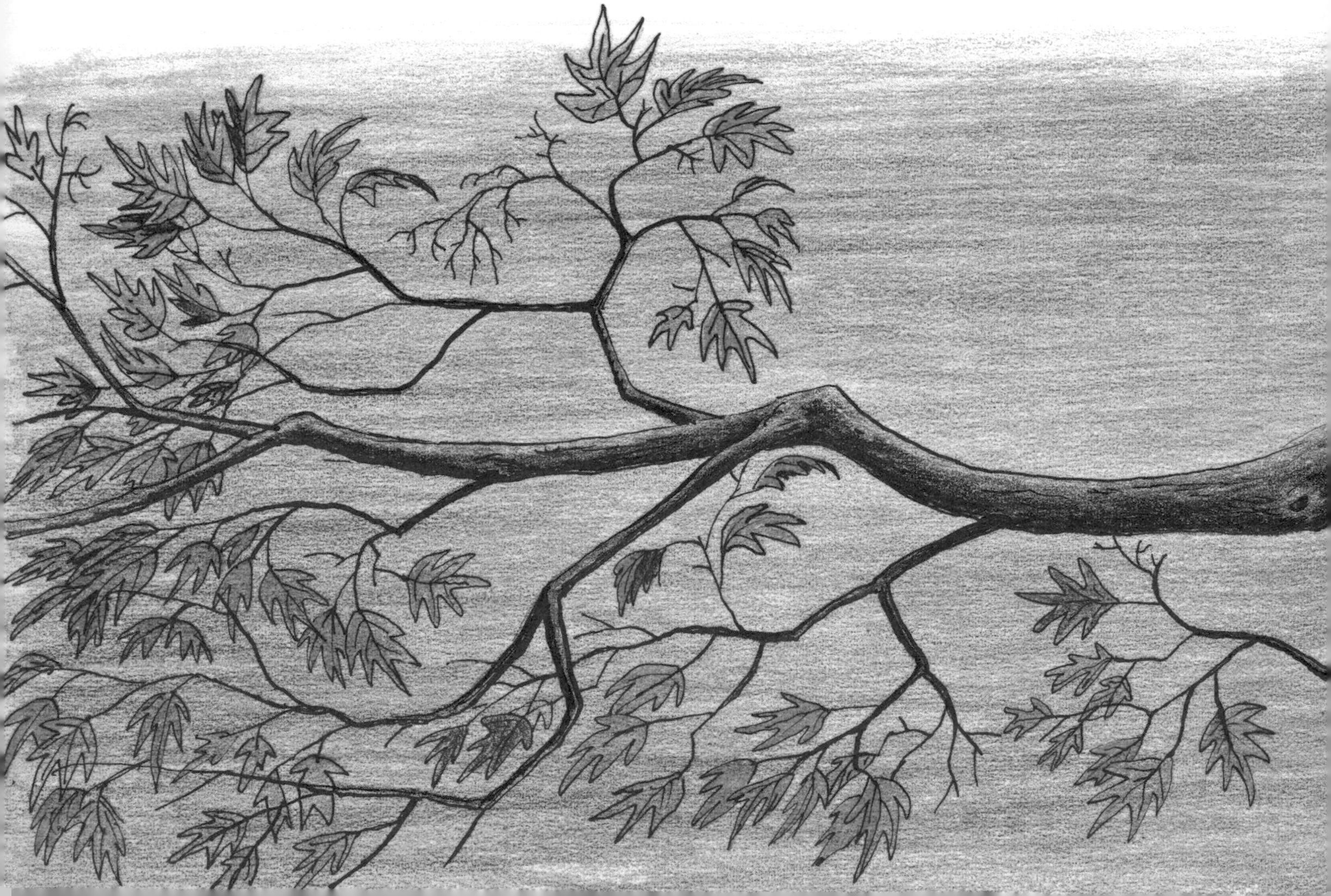

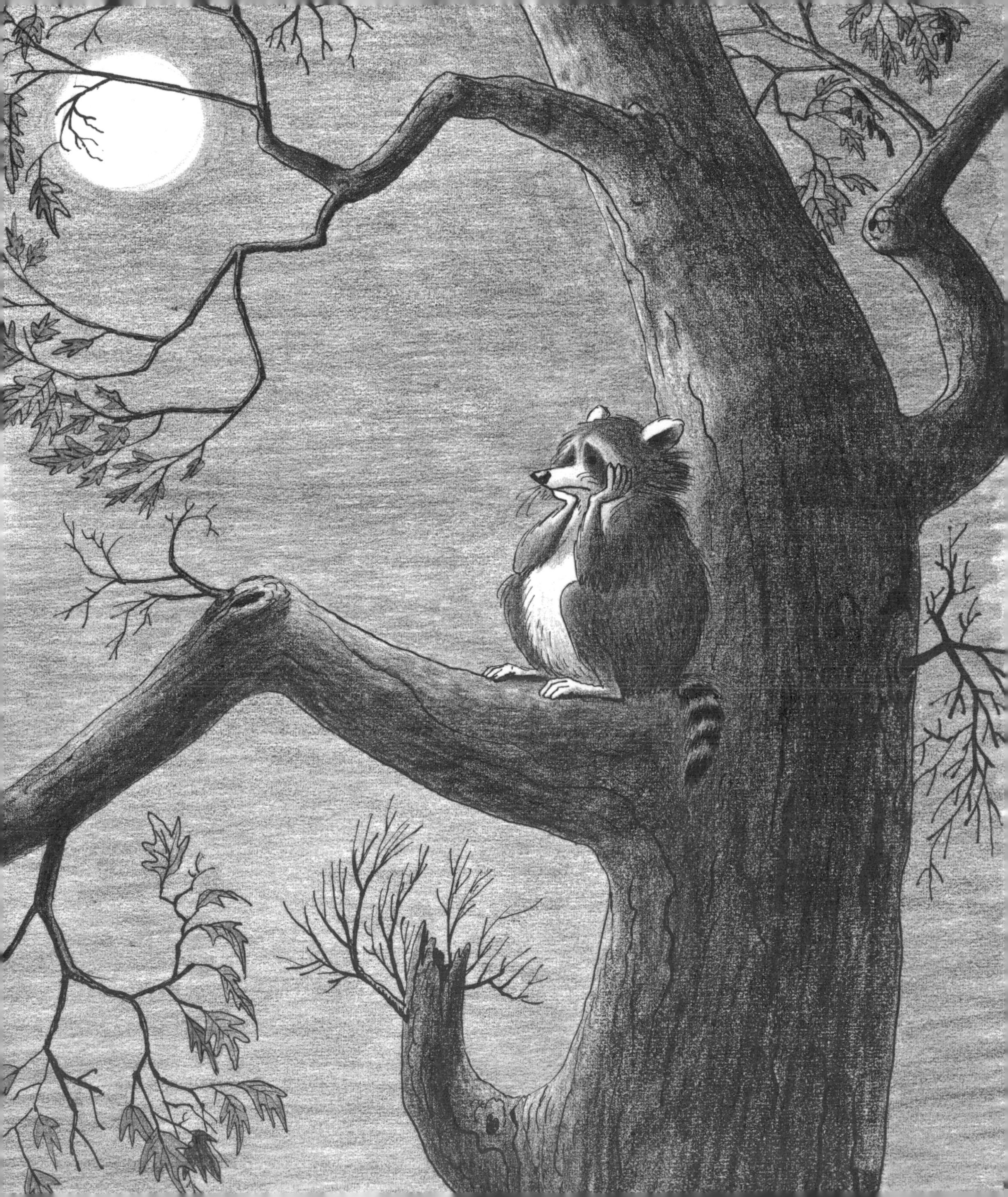

Early the next morning the raccoon called his friends together. "There's no time to lose," he warned. "We must leave Shady Glade at once and go far far away. Not just a little way, hundreds of miles away where the monsters will never catch up with us."

"But where?" whimpered a rabbit.

"We won't know until we get there."

"And how do we go," boomed the bullfrog, "fly?"

"We take the train."

This left them wide-eyed and speechless, so the raccoon quickly explained, "We'll board the train from the sycamore," and pointed to a limb that went twisting high above the creek and up over the railroad trestle.

"Not me," boomed the bullfrog. "I'll take my chances right here." Then he leaped into the creek *kerplop!* and his five friends followed with a *plink! plink! plink! plink! plink!*

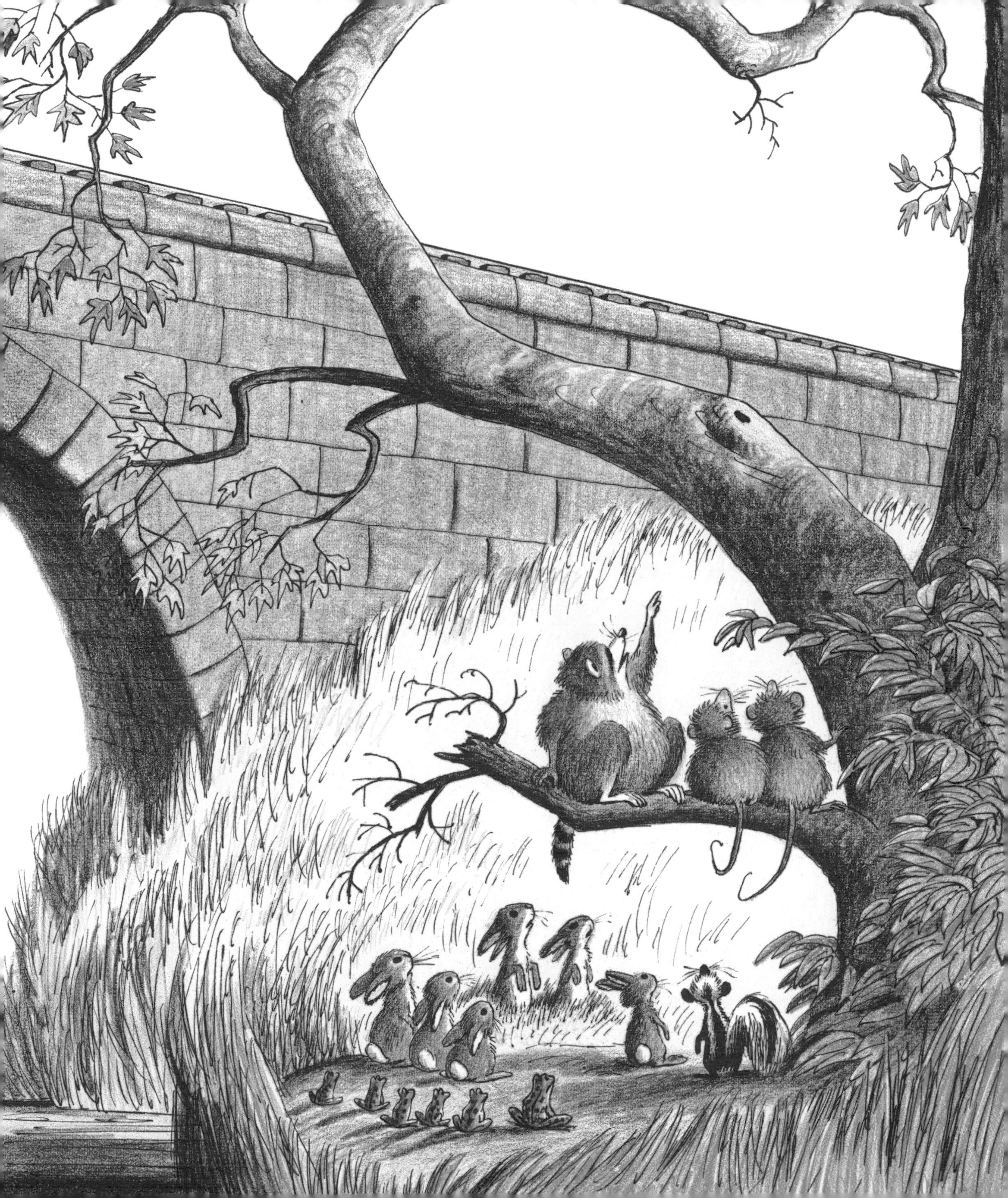

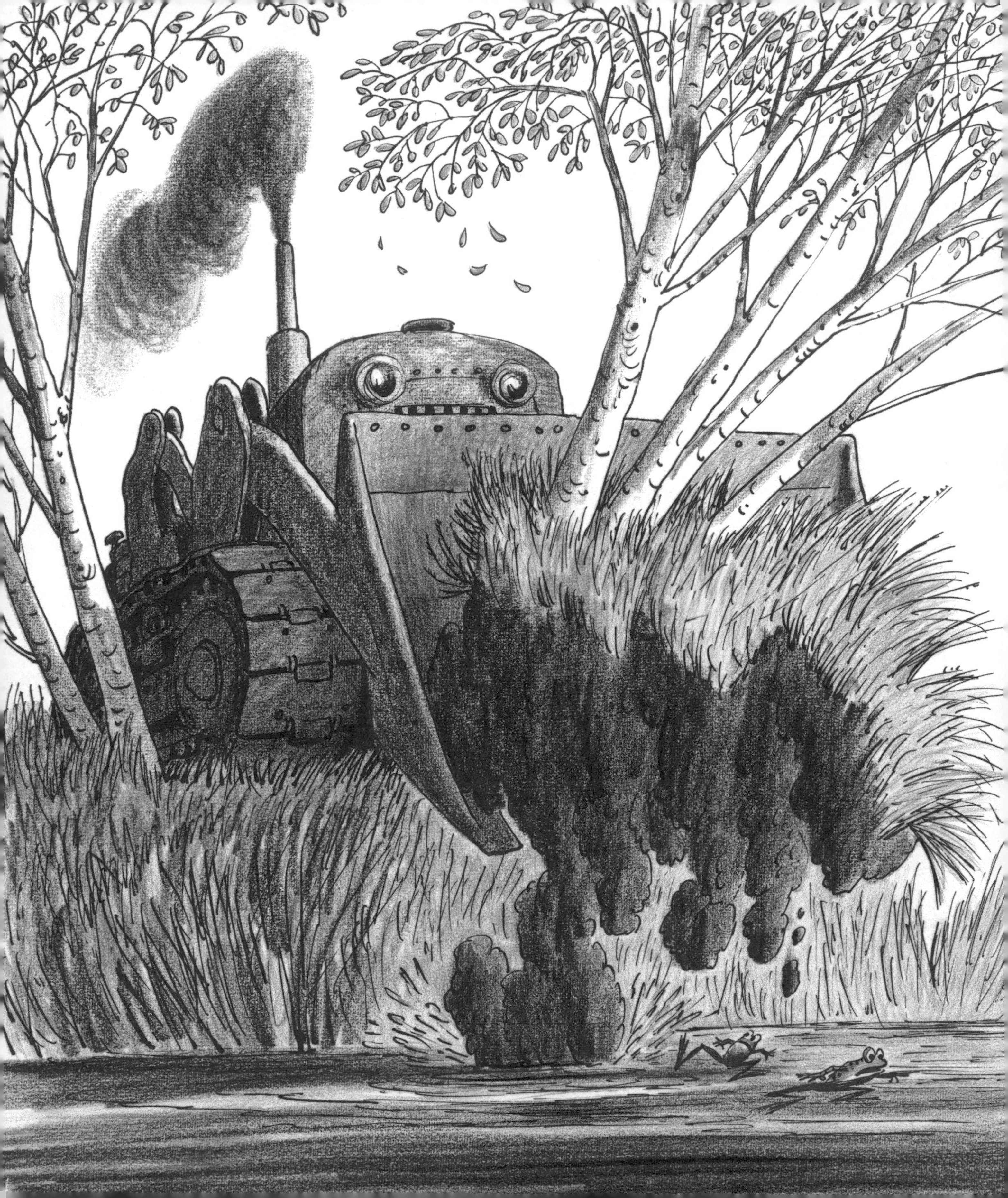

The rest were all eager and ready to go and as the raccoon waddled up the limb they were close at his heels. Halfway up they were startled by a thundering roar as a giant bulldozer came crashing through the glade sending an avalanche of earth and tree limbs tumbling into the creek. The frogs barely escaped. In a pop-eyed panic they came leaping onto the bank and went hopping up the sycamore to join the others.

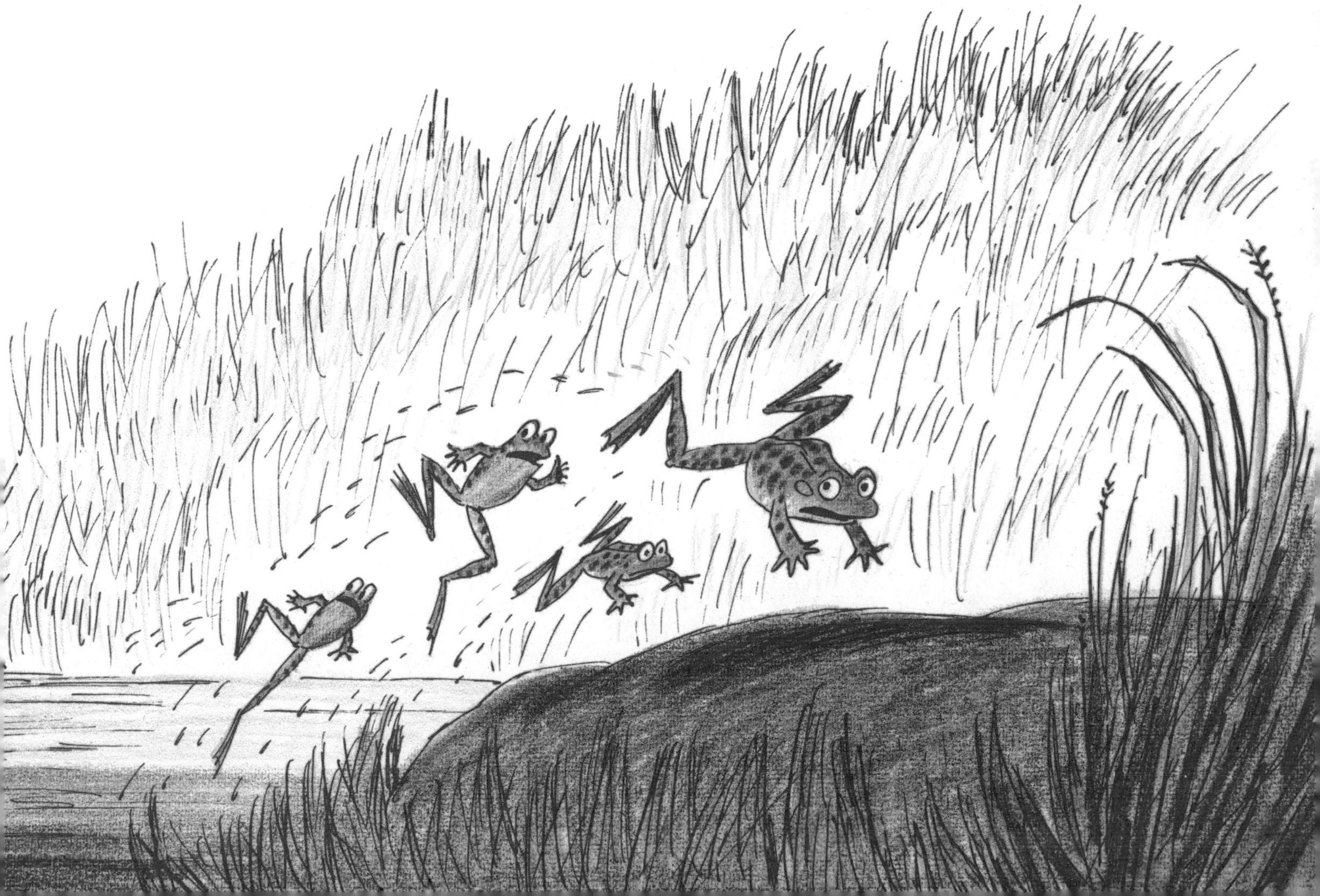

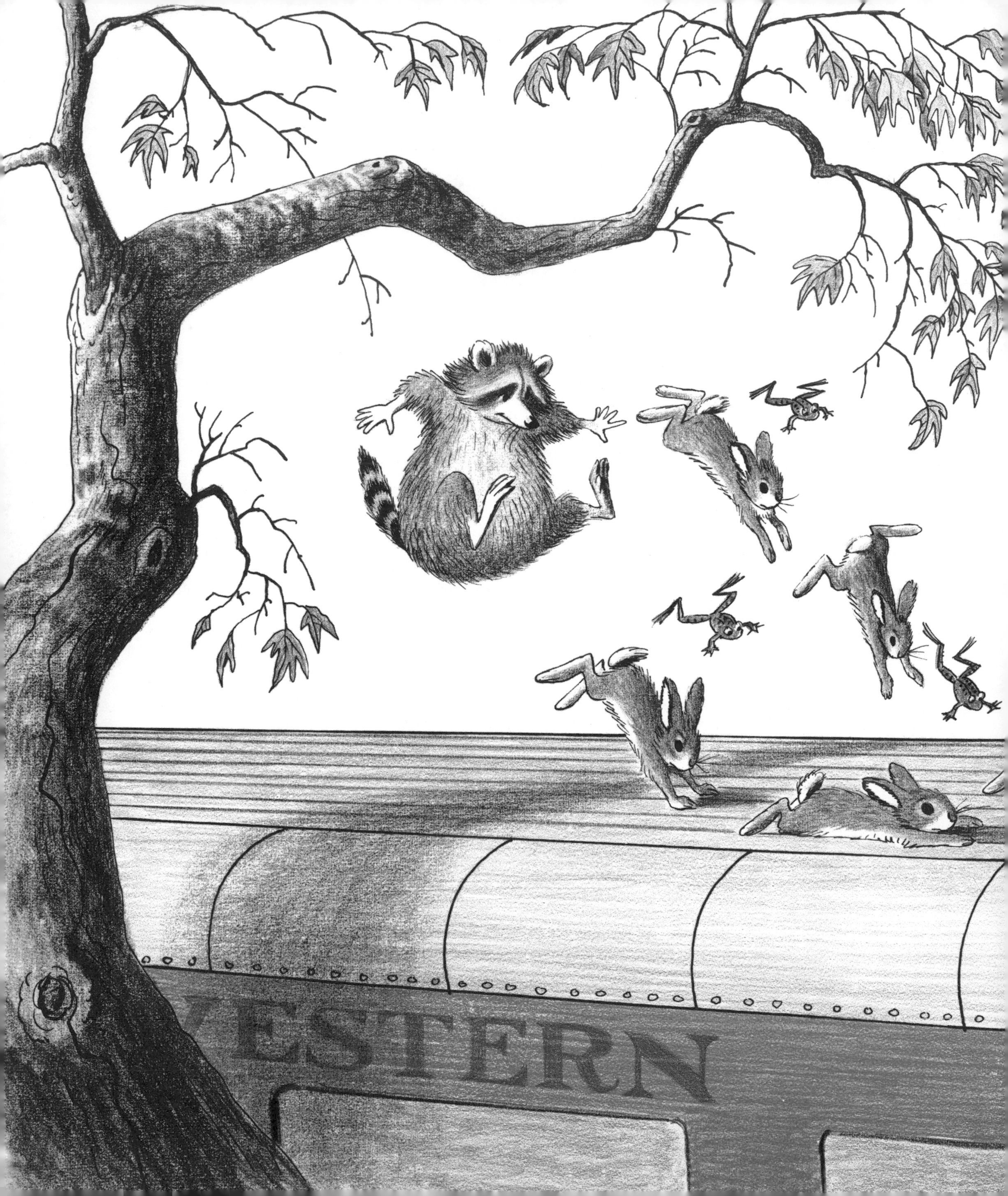
ESTERN

They were all no sooner bunched together over the trestle when a train whistle sounded above the roaring bulldozer.

"Now don't jump until I give the signal," shouted the raccoon, "and when you land, remember to land flat!"

When the diesel locomotive came rushing under them, the raccoon raised a finger — "Get set!" — and as the streamlined cars flashed by he gave the signal — "All aboard!" — and they jumped, each one in a perfectly flat four point landing. Everyone but the roly-poly raccoon who hit with a big bounce and nearly rolled off before he caught himself. Then he turned for one last farewell look at Shady Glade, a fleeting glimpse of the sycamore as the great tree toppled and disappeared in a billowing cloud of dust.

In a very few minutes the streamliner was streaking along at top speed out in the open countryside. The rolling farmland stretched on and on, mile after mile, wheat fields and cornfields and barbed wire fences as far as the eye could see. Now and then they spied a clump of trees beside a creek and a patch of woods here and there, but if these places were anything like Shady Glade it was hard to tell. They went flashing by much too quickly.

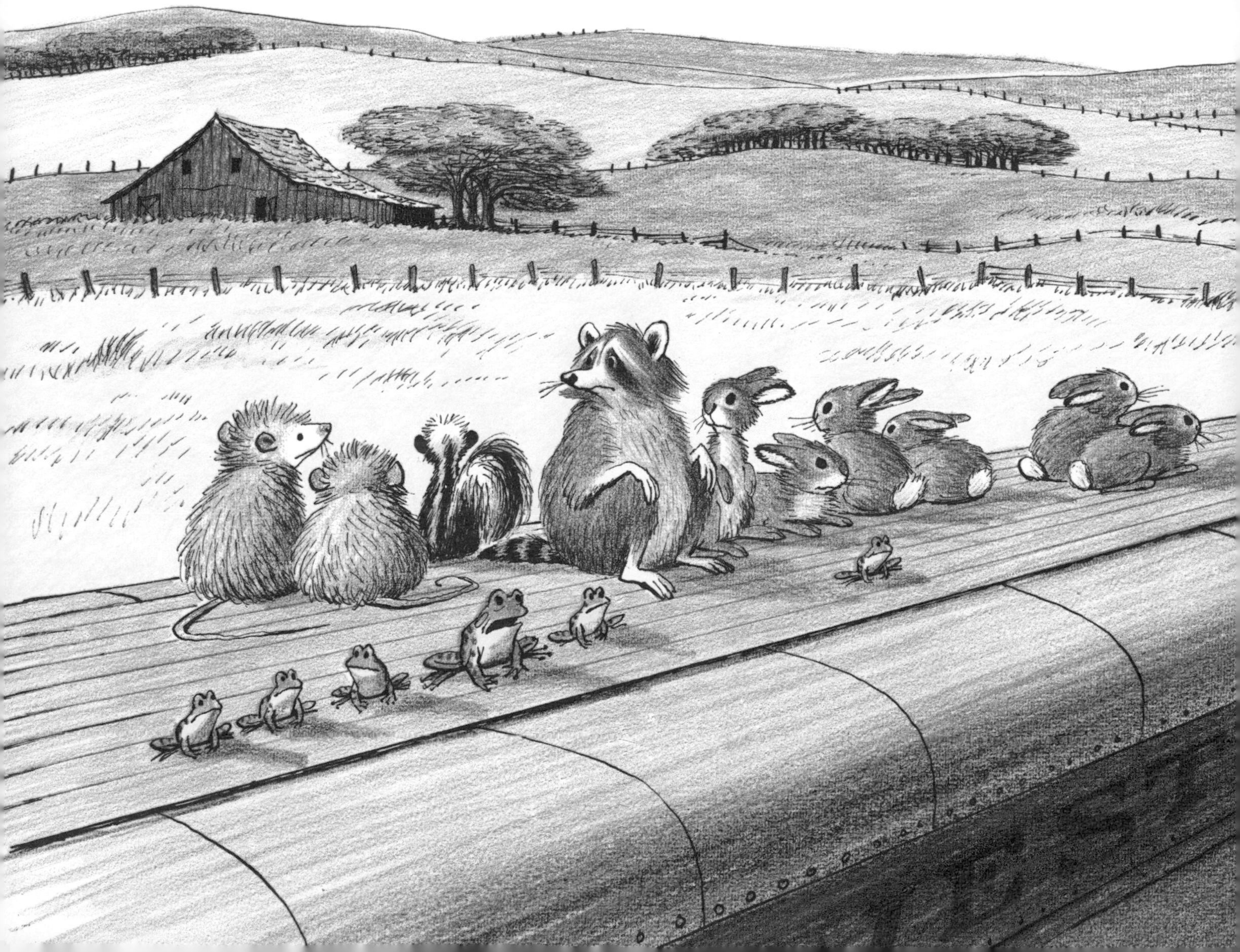

"If we should find a likely spot," grumbled the bullfrog, "do we take a flying leap off the train and break every bone?"

The raccoon didn't answer, for that was the very thing he was worried about.

"Well, I know one thing," continued the frog. "This train won't stop until it comes to a big city. I'll bet a hind leg on that!"

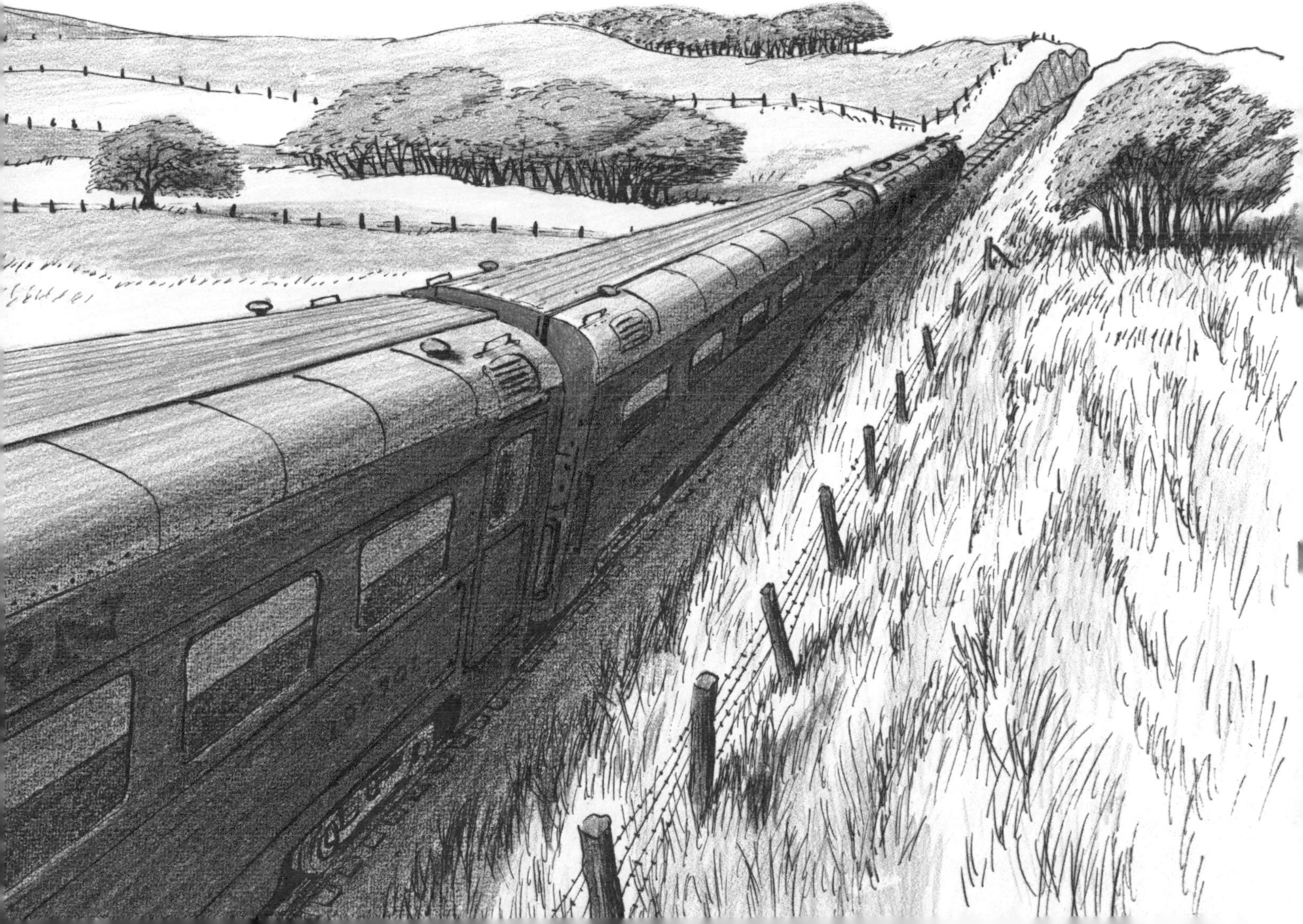

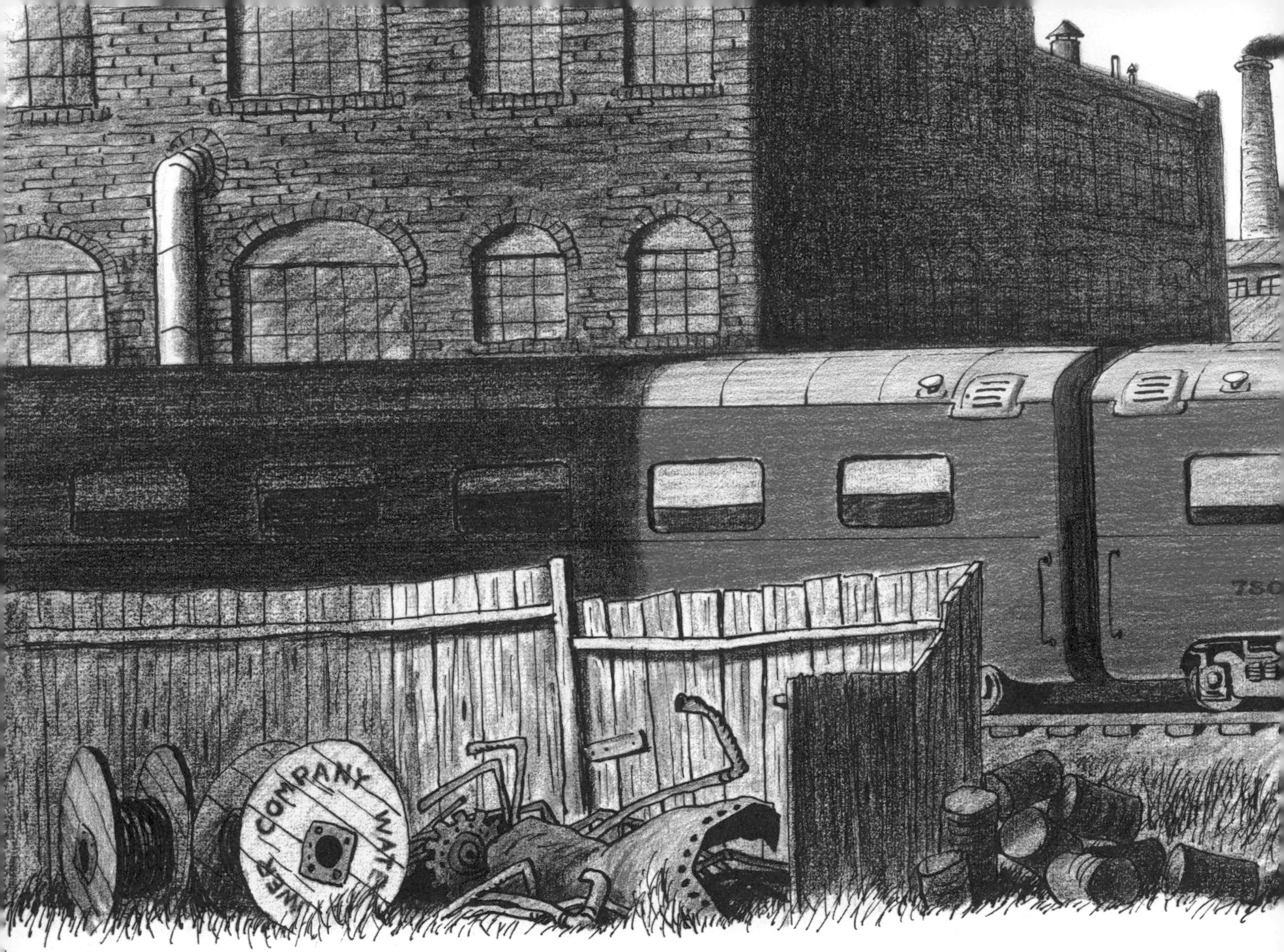
COMPANY

The bullfrog was right. Late in the afternoon the streamliner gradually began to slow down. Pretty soon it was moving at a crawl past junkyards and factories on the way into a big city. As the train rumbled over a viaduct the bullfrog bellowed, "There's a creek for you! Anyone for a swim?!"

At one time it *had* been a creek, crystal clear and shaded by willows. Now its banks were steep cement walls with pipes spouting purple-green waste from the factory buildings into the scummy water.

"What a sorry sight," sighed the old raccoon.

"What a stench," squeeked the skunk.

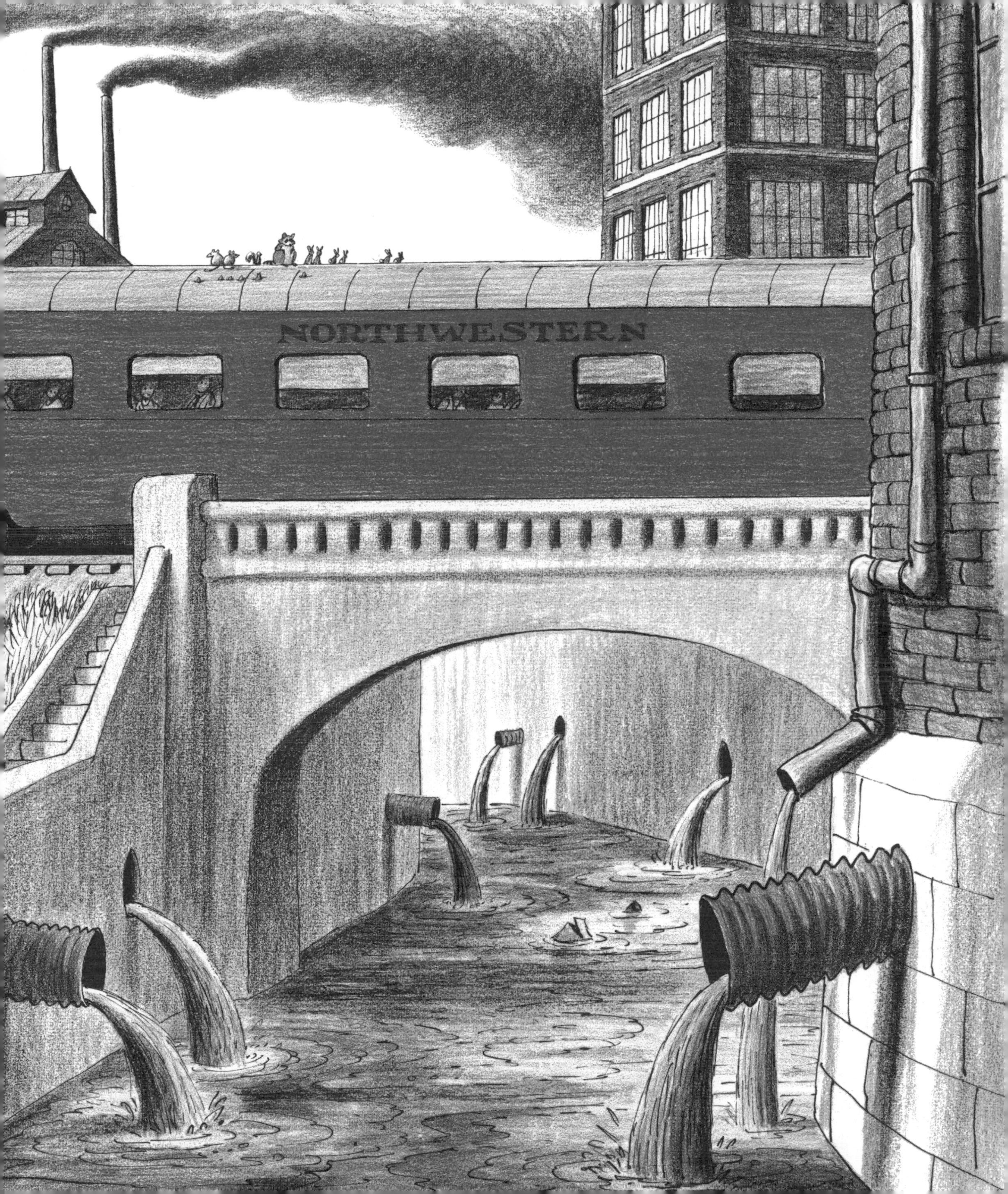
NORTHWESTERN

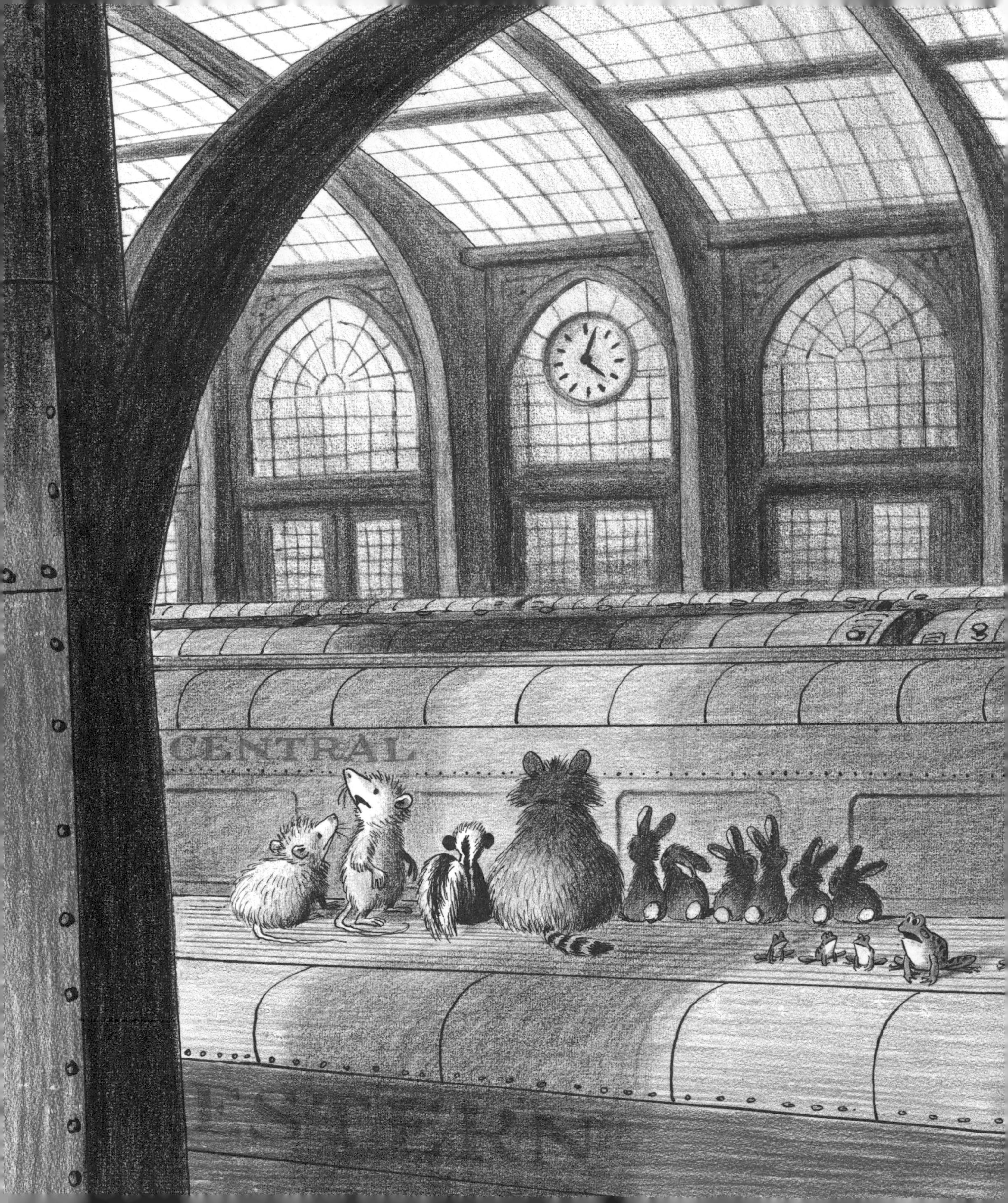
CENTRAL

The train crept slower and slower until it finally shuddered to a stop in the eerie gloom of a cavernous railroad station.

"I have a hunch this is the end of the line," boomed the bullfrog, "and the end of us too."

"All we can do," replied the raccoon, "is wait and see."

They waited while the station clock ticked away an hour, and they watched the people crowding on and off the coaches. Streamliners kept coming and going, but still their train gave no sign of moving, and it appeared that once again the bullfrog was right, when suddenly the conductor shouted "All aboard! All aboard!" The coaches jerked forward and the train rumbled out of the station and on across the city gaining speed as it went, until once more they were streaking along in the open countryside.

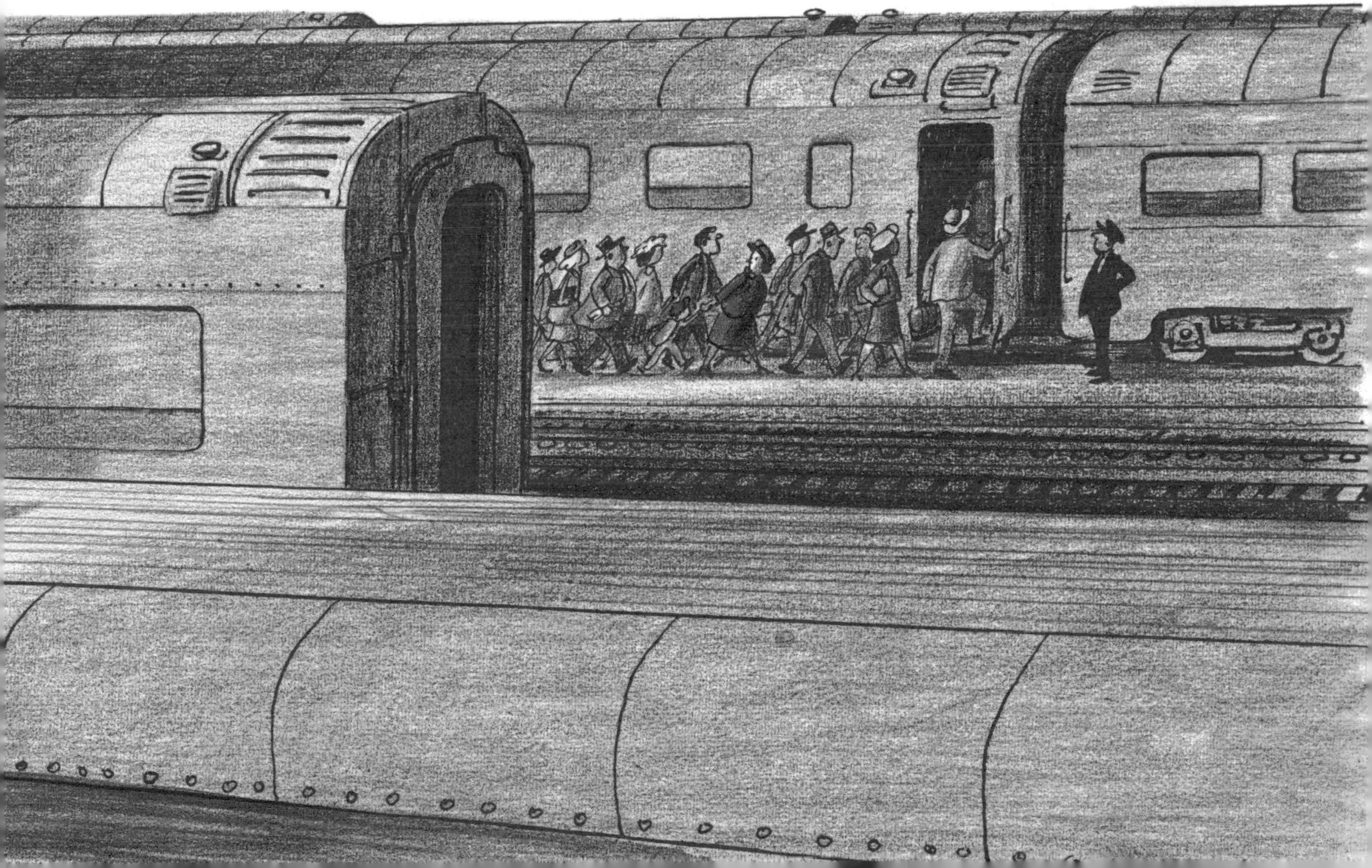

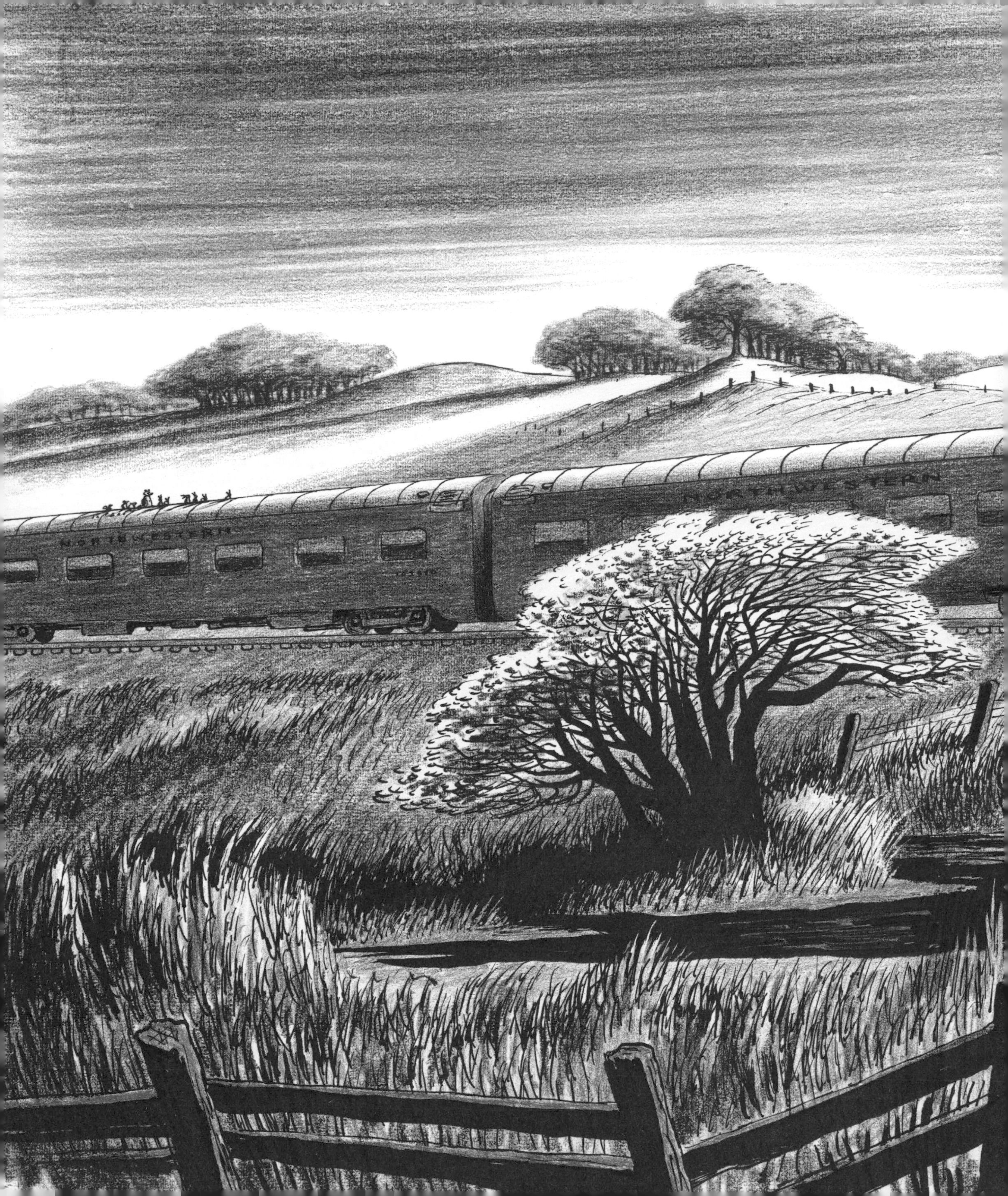
NORTHWESTERN
NORTHWESTERN

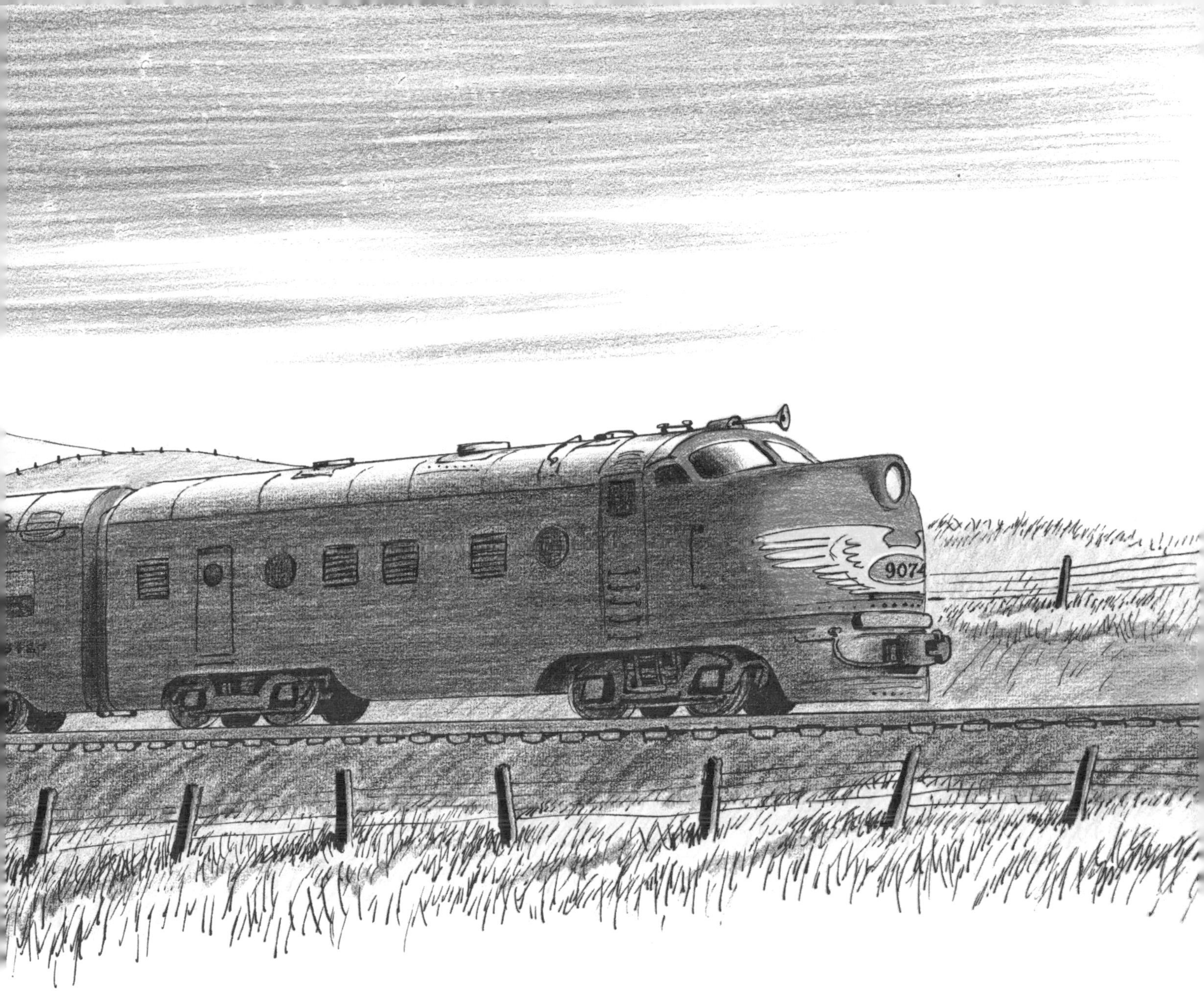
9074

As the miles went rolling by through the long afternoon the scenery began to change. Now the farmland was hilly with more and more trees and the old raccoon's beady eyes brightened with renewed hope. His friends didn't seem to notice. They were too travel-weary and drowsy to care, and one by one they dropped off to sleep.

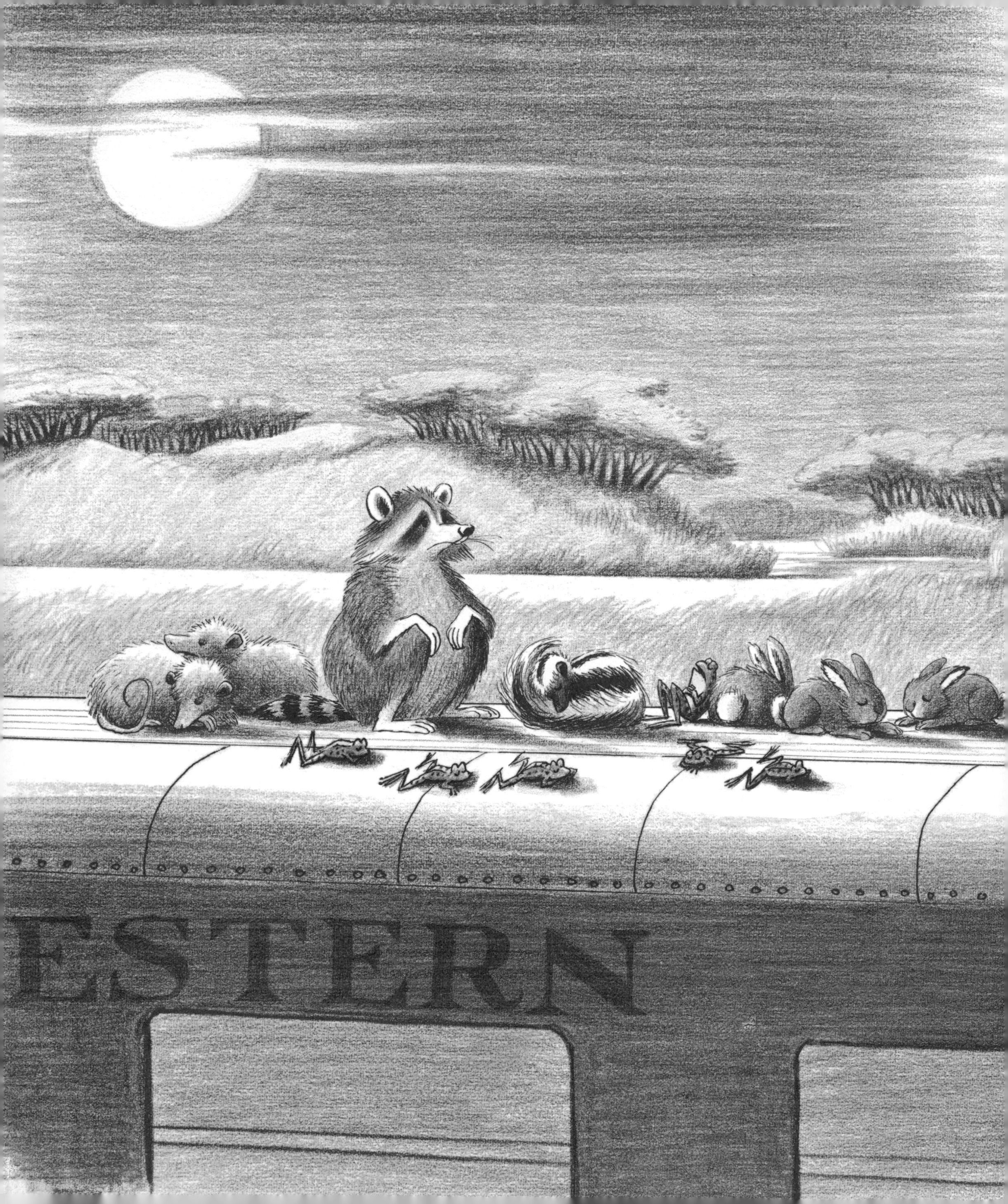
ESTERN

The streamliner raced on through the evening then on into the night, past miles and miles of dense forest and winding streams, a thousand Shady Glades rolled into one, and only a few jumps away. But that first jump was impossible.

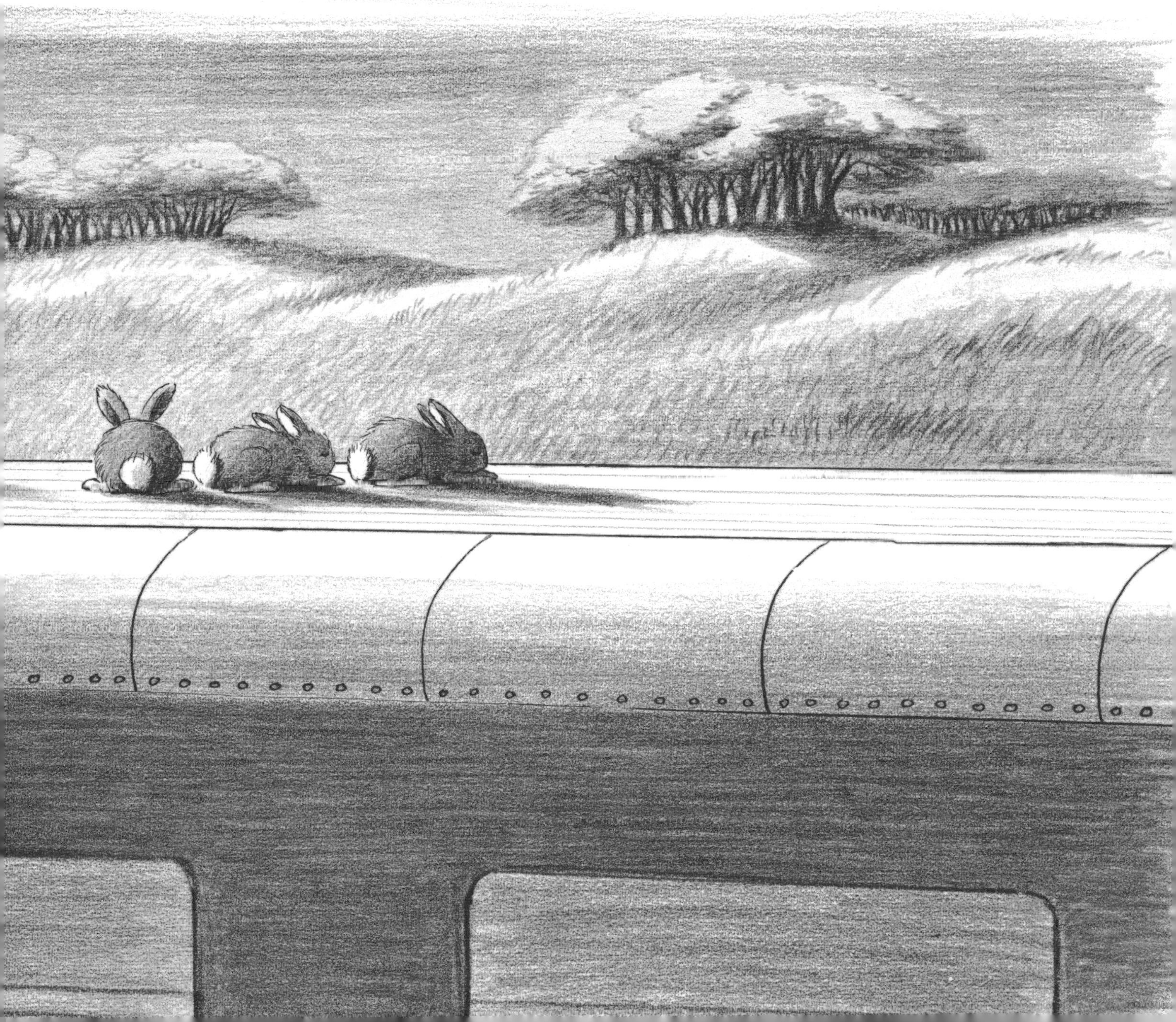

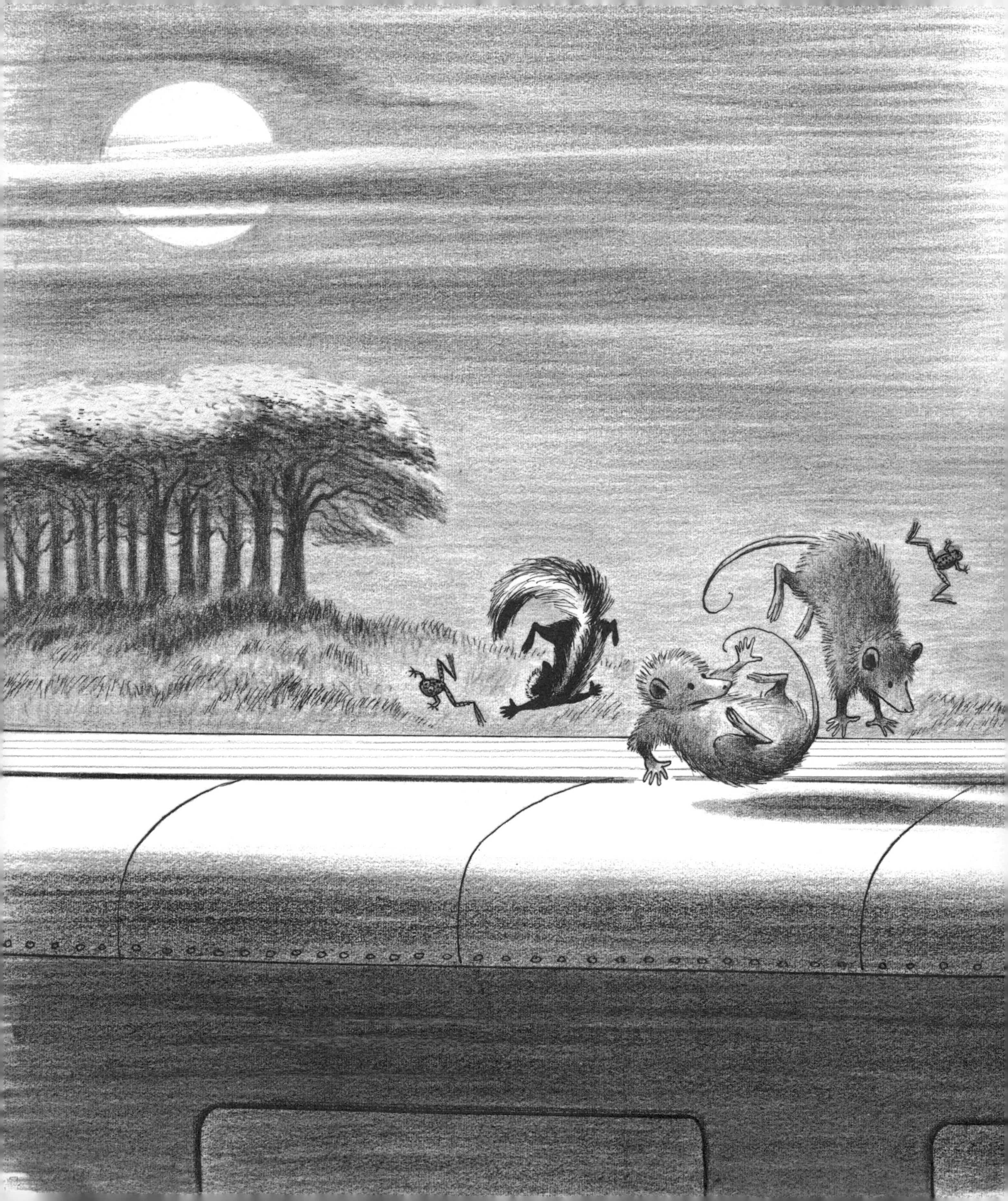

At last the weary raccoon decided to join his friends. He curled himself into a fuzzy ball and was just about to doze off when suddenly there was a screeching of wheels! A hissing of brakes! Then a thundering *boom* as all the cars came jolting together. The raccoon, the rabbits, the possums, the skunk and the frogs went skidding and tumbling halfway down the car to pile up in a heap. Then there was silence.

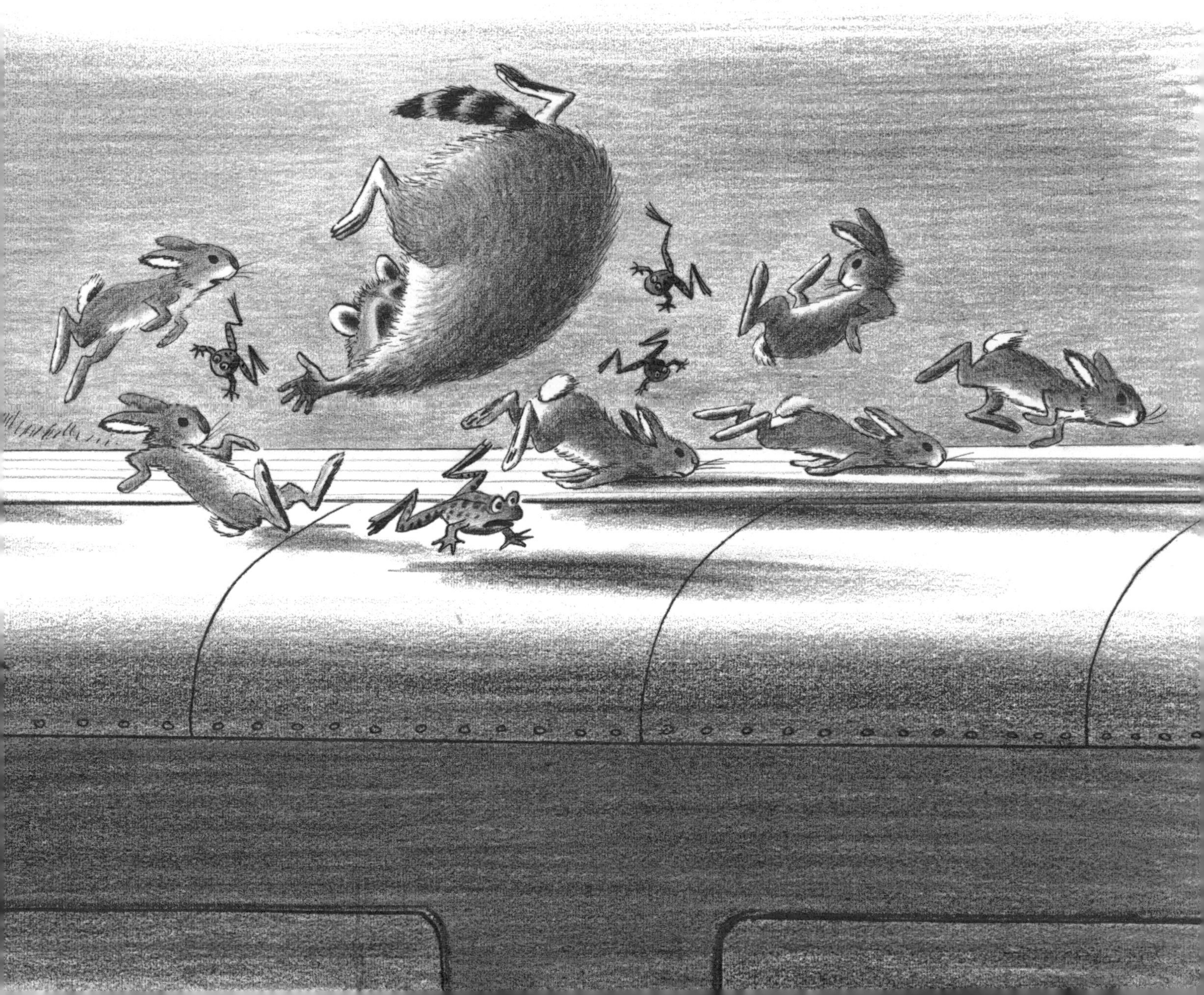

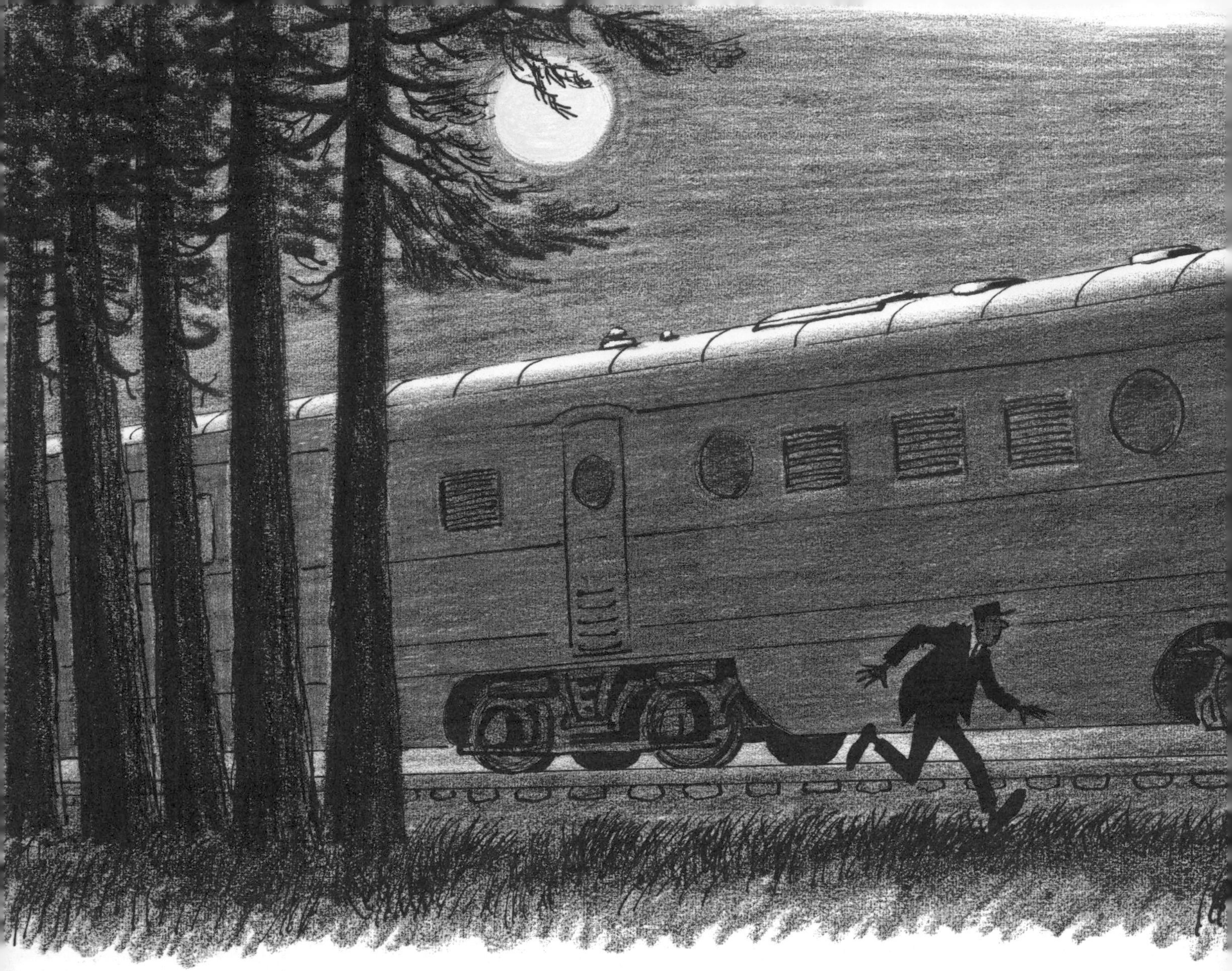

The train had stopped. Pretty soon excited voices echoed into the dense woods alongside the track.

"What's up?" "What happened?" "What is it?" "What's it all about?"

"A rock slide," growled the engineer. "Lucky we got her stopped in time."

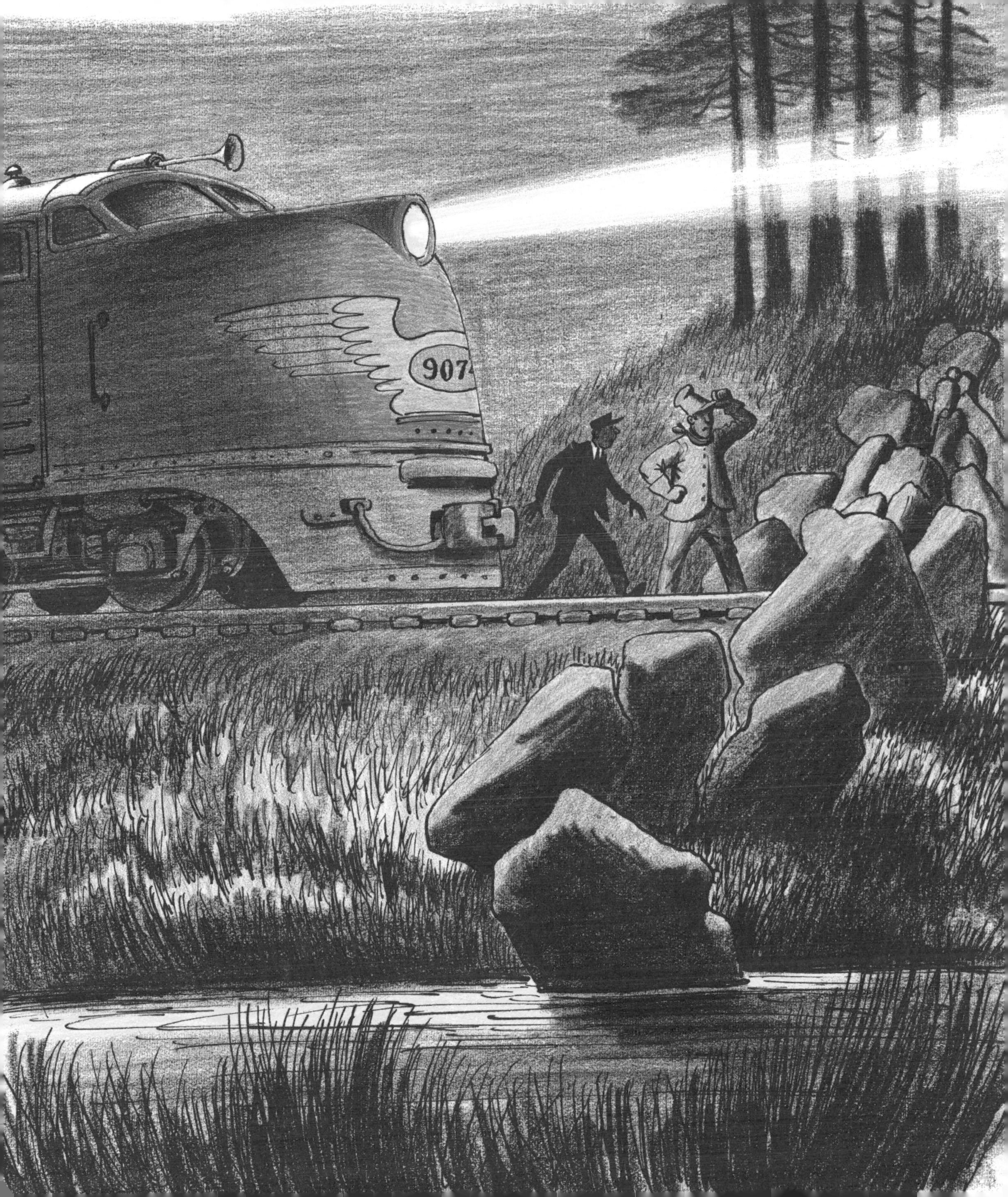
907

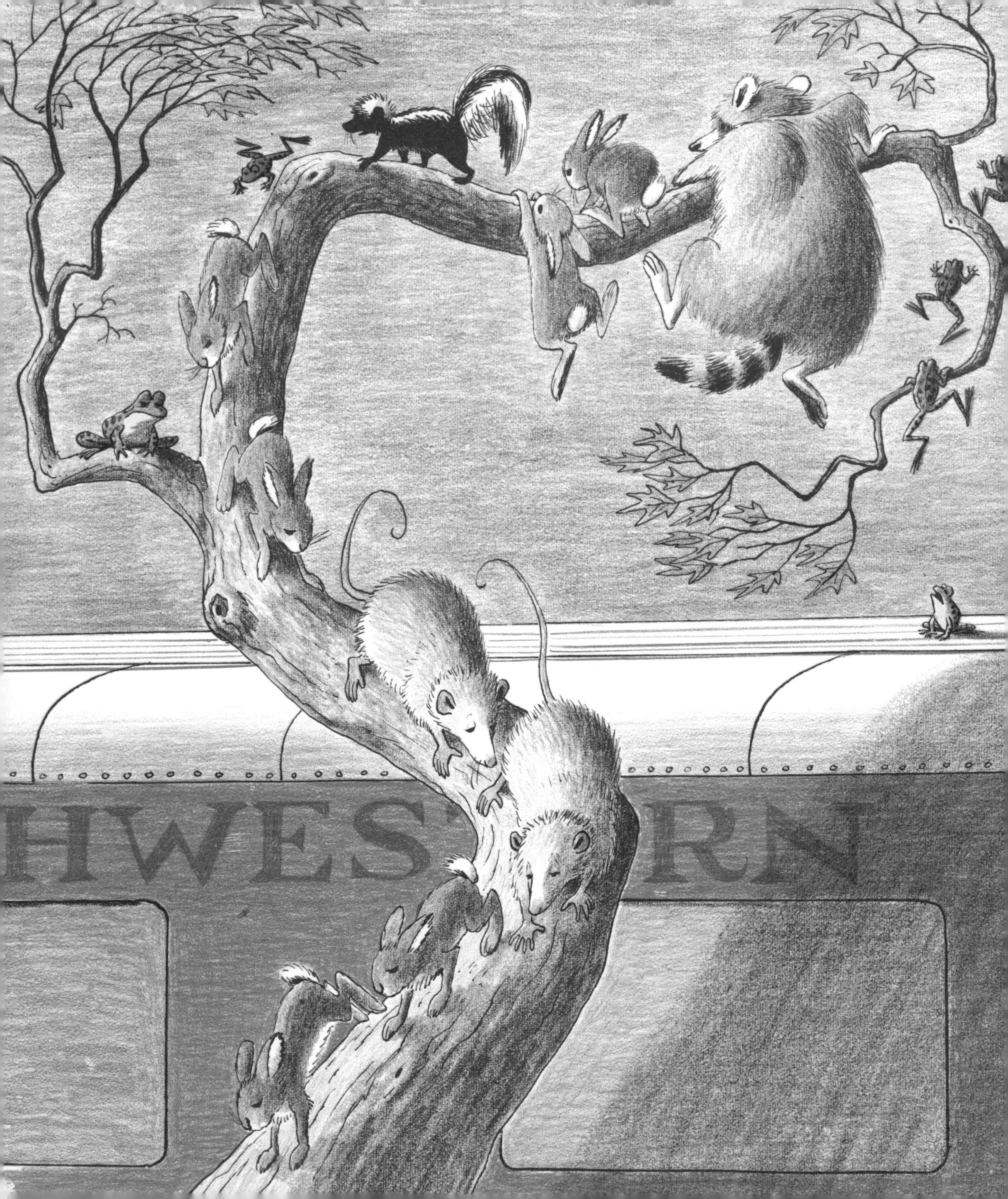
HWES RN

"More trouble," grumbled the bullfrog.

"No trouble at all," chortled the raccoon pointing to a twisting sycamore limb just a few feet above the roof of the streamliner — "Last stop everybody! All off! End of the line!" — and the sleepy-eyed passengers from Shady Glade went trooping down the treelimb. Somewhere below in the darkness they huddled together to finish their night's sleep.

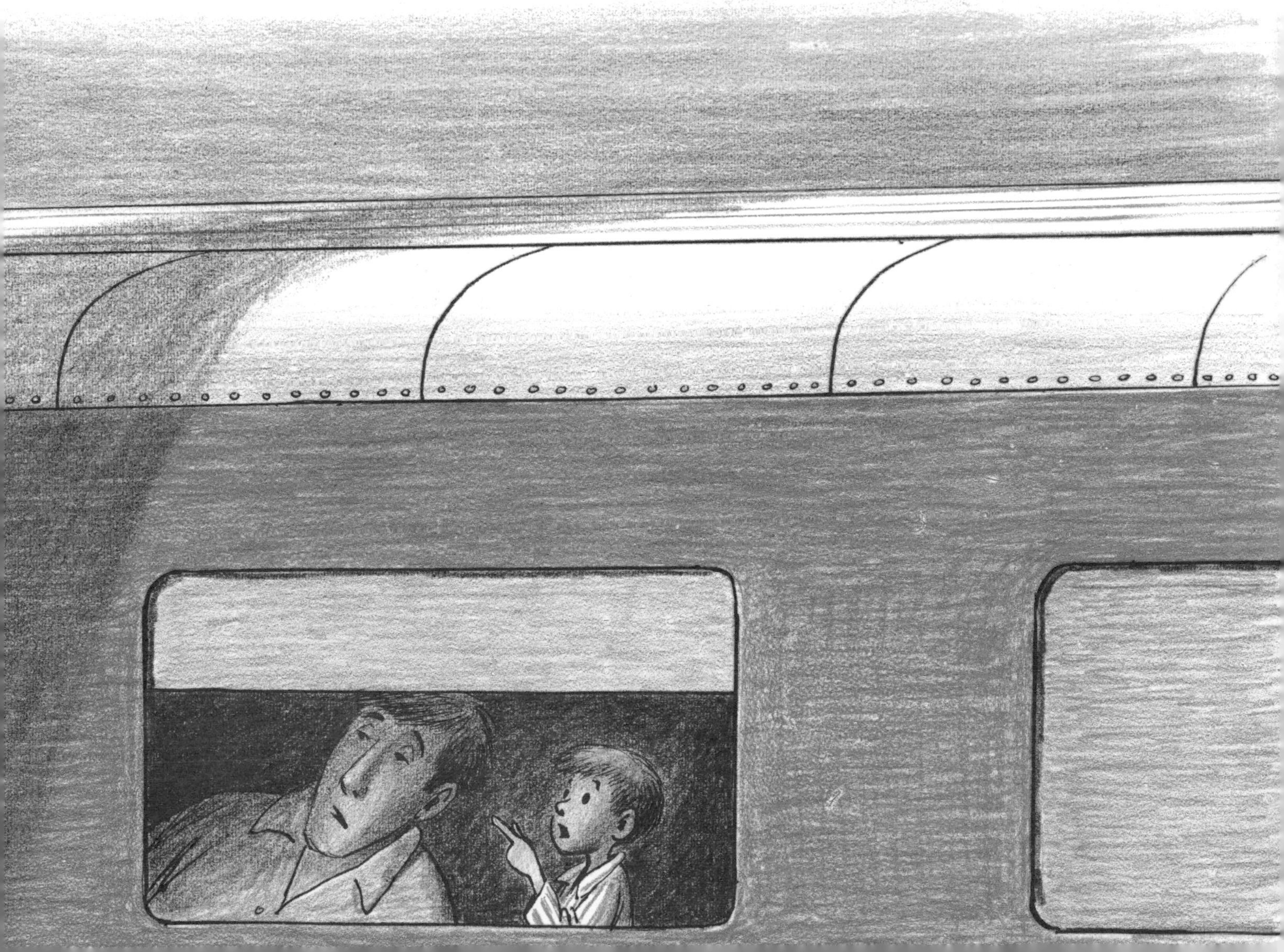

The next morning when they awakened for their first view of the new surroundings they were overjoyed.

"This is more like it," boomed the bullfrog.

"Exactly like it," exclaimed the raccoon. For it was indeed almost exactly like Shady Glade with a towering sycamore, a winding creek, and all the trimmings. And to their horror there was even that same deep rumbling sound. The trees trembled to their very roots and the creek shivered in its banks.

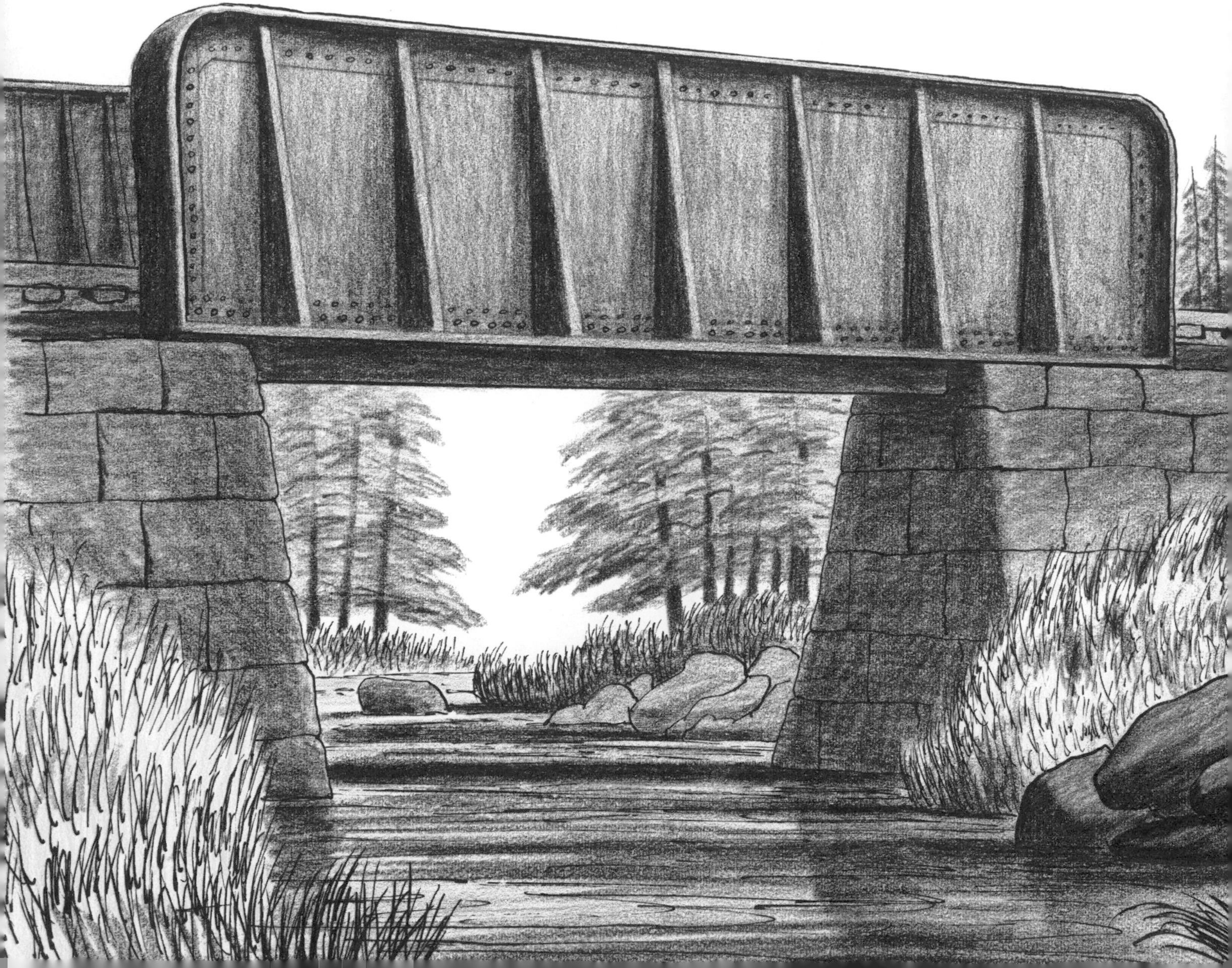

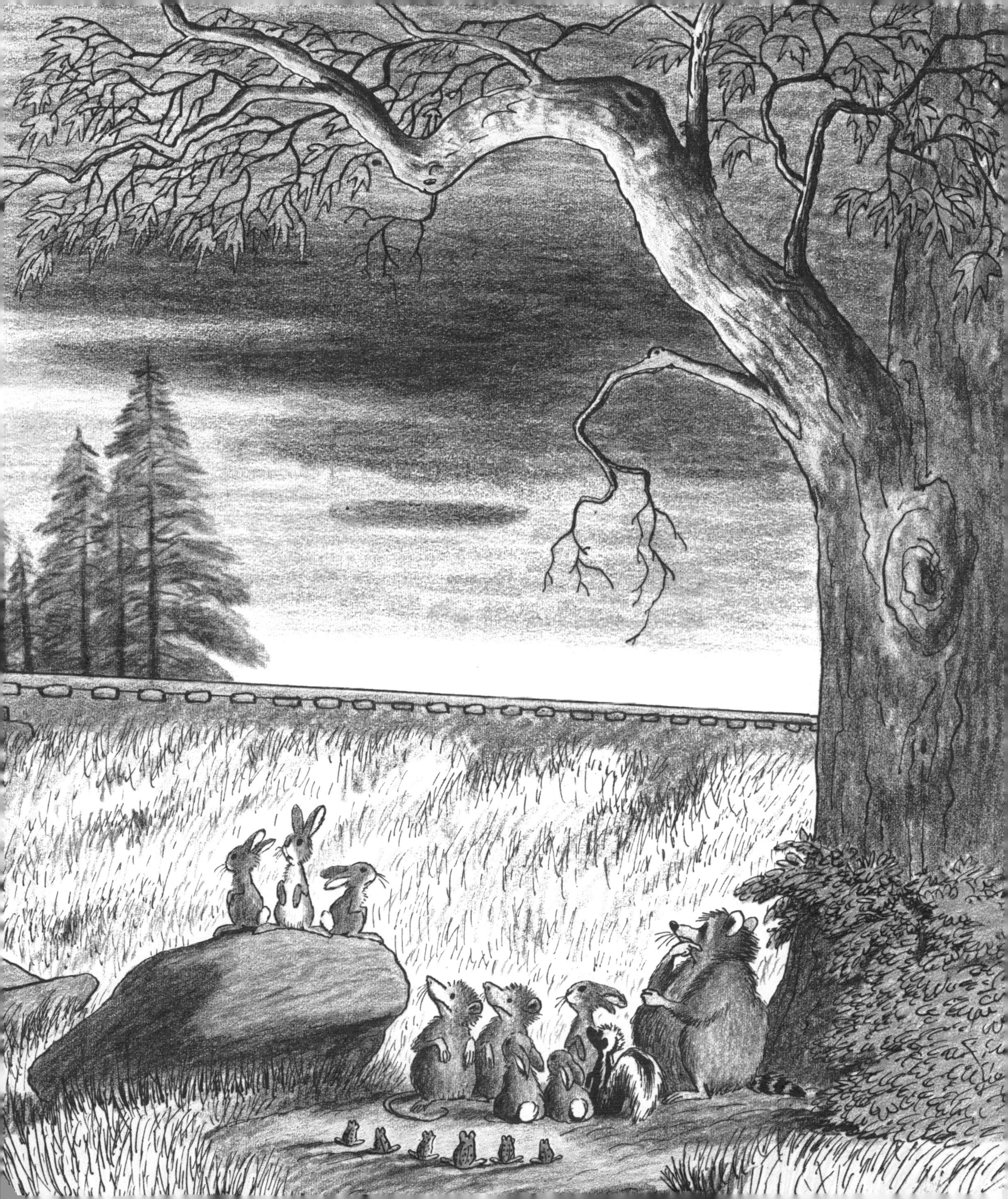

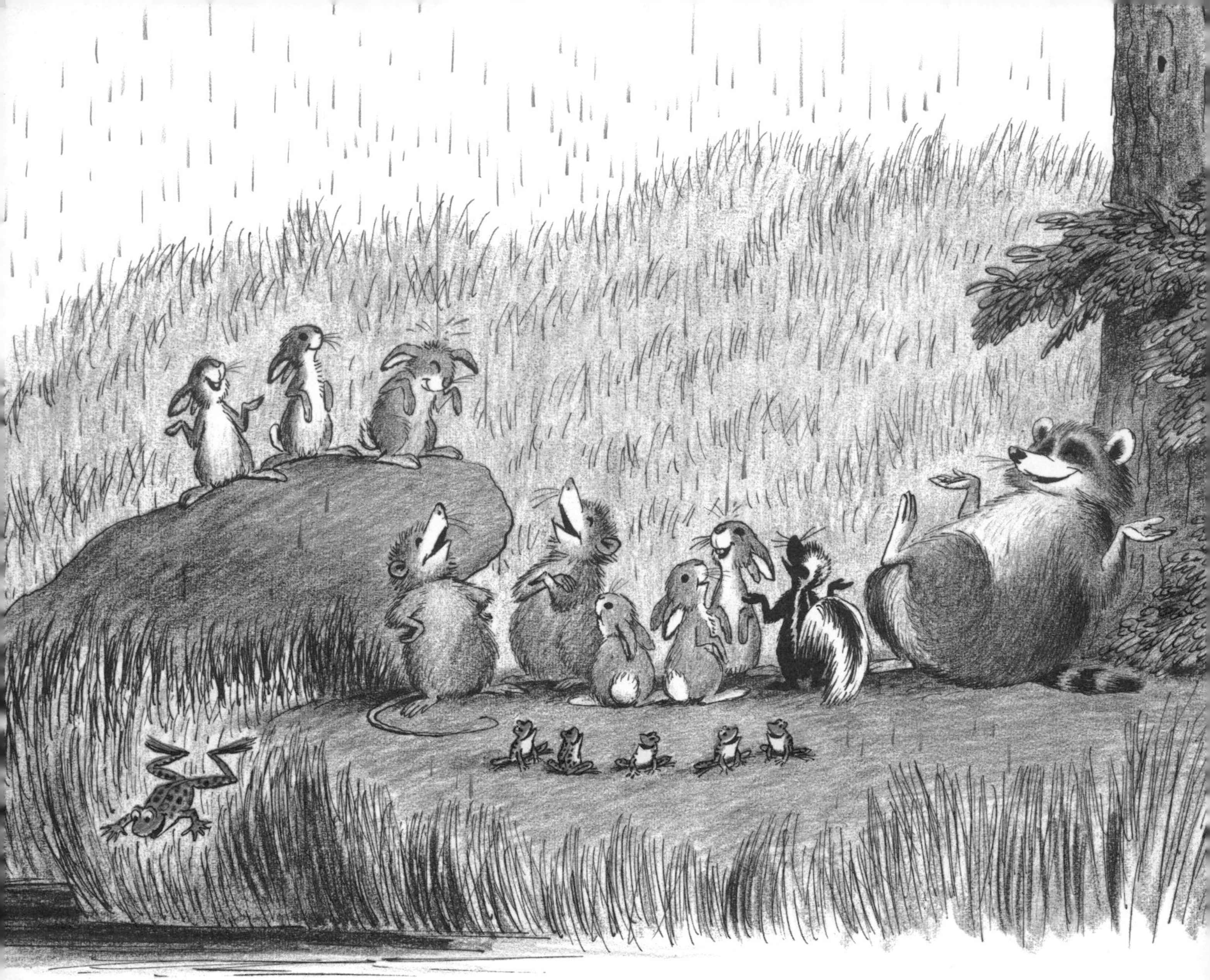

"It's not a train," muttered the raccoon peering up at the railroad trestle. "But it could very well be thunder," he said pointing to the rain clouds high overhead. There was a flicker of lightning, then more deep rumbling, and a gentle rain began to fall.

"A little bit of rain never hurt anyone," said the bullfrog as he *kerplopped* into the creek.

"You're perfectly right," smiled the happy raccoon. "In fact, everything is perfectly right."